D0092961

WHERE THREE ROADS MEET

BOOKS BY JOHN BARTH

THE FLOATING OPERA

THE END OF THE ROAD

THE SOT-WEED FACTOR

GILES GOAT-BOY

LOST IN THE FUNHOUSE: FICTION FOR PRINT, TAPE, LIVE VOICE

CHIMERA

LETTERS

SABBATICAL: A ROMANCE

the slope-shouldered spirit of his erstwhile Helper. "The odds against him are about the same as against any given *motile* spermatozoon, even. And he's got so *fucking* much yet to learn!"

Granted, Al. Nor is he one of your capital-H Heroes, for sure.

All the same (concludes the Three Freds Story), *he's going to try.*

THE FRIDAY BOOK: ESSAYS AND OTHER NONFICTION

THE TIDEWATER TALES: A NOVEL

THE LAST VOYAGE OF SOMEBODY THE SAILOR

ONCE UPON A TIME: A FLOATING OPERA

FURTHER FRIDAYS: ESSAYS, LECTURES, AND OTHER NONFICTION, 1984–1994

ON WITH THE STORY

COMING SOON!!!

THE BOOK OF TEN NIGHTS AND A NIGHT: ELEVEN STORIES

WHERE THREE ROADS MEET: NOVELLAS

JOHN BARTH

HOUGHTON MIFFLIN COMPANY

WHERE THREE ROADS MEET

Novellas

BOSTON / NEW YORK / 2005

Visit our Web site: www.houghtonmifflinbooks.com.

Library of Congress Cataloging-in-Publication Data

Barth, John, date.

Where three roads meet : novellas / John Barth.

p. cm.

Contents: Tell me—I've been told—As I was saying . . .

ISBN-13: 978-0-618-61016-7

ISBN-10: 0-618-61016-2

I. Title.

PS3552.A75W47 2005

813'.54—dc22 2005040325

Book design by Melissa Lotfy

Printed in the United States of America

QUM 10 9 8 7 6 5 4 3 2 1

"Tell Me" first appeared in the Spring 2005 issue of *Fiction*. "I've Been Told" first appeared, in slightly different form, in *Conjunctions* 44, also in Spring 2005.

I'VE BEEN TOLD: A STORY'S STORY

II

FOR SHELLY

CONTENTS

I

TELL ME

IF AND WHEN he ever gets his narrative shit together, Will Chase might tell the Story of the Three Freds more or less like this—freely changing names, roles, settings, and any other elements large or small as his by-then-more-seasoned muse sees fit, neither to protect the innocent nor to shield the blamable, but simply to make the tale more tellworthy:

1. THE CALL

Mid-spring mid-morning in mid-twentieth-century USA—in the mid-Atlantic-coast state of Maryland, to be exact, and even in mid-sentence, as our then young and recently interrupted narrator made to resume his anecdote-in-progress by saying to his apartment-mates, "As I was saying, guys"—their telephone rang again.

"Your turn," his friend Al said to their friend Winnie: a standing joke between that latter pair (although both were in fact seated, on their hand-me-down couch in their grad-student apartment in the university's high-rise Briarwood Residences, just off campus), inasmuch as in those days before phone-answering machines, Winnie, Al's girlfriend, took all their calls, for reasons presently to be explained, and thus had taken the previously interruptive one (wrong number) a few minutes before. With a roll of her eyes she reached again for the phone—one of those black rotary-dial jobs, standard issue back then—on the hand-me-down end table next to which she customarily sat, when reading or chatting, for just that purpose.

"Hello?"

"If this were a story and you were its narrator," Alfred Baumann advised Wilfred Chase while Winifred Stark attended the caller, "you could stop the action right here and get some capital-E Exposition done: like who the Three Freds are and what they're doing here; what the capital-C Conflict is; what's At Stake for whichever of us is the Protagonist, and why Win takes all our calls in Briarwood Three-oh-four . . ."

Roger wilco, old buddy, as even callow nonveterans like themselves sometimes said in those postwar days: military radio-communications lingo for *Got your message and will comply.* Post–World War Two is the *when* of this story, although the nation's brief peaceful respite after V-J Day 1945 would end in 1950 with North Korea's invasion of South and the American-run UN "police action" to contain that invasion. Excuse Narrator if you knew all that, Reader: It matters because this story's *where* is the campus environs of a major university—a campus swarming, as were all such in the USA back then, with veterans of that previous war, their educations subsidized by the GI Bill of Rights. At all-male institutions such as this was in those days, the undergraduate student body was thus divided into somewhat older, more life-experienced, and now draft-exempt World War Two vets, many of them married, and younger, greener, soon-to-be-draft-vulnerable hands like the then Will Chase and his only slightly older best friend and mentor, Al Baumann.

Greener, yes, in that neither Al nor Will had shared their war-veteran classmates' transformative experience of military service, not to mention actual combat. But green comes in shades, and in every other respect Al was so much the savvier that as of this telling Narrator still shakes his head at that pair's friendship, wondering what on earth Al B. found interesting in Will C.; what *he* got from a connection so clearly beneficial to his protégé. Born and raised in one of the city's most desirable neighborhoods as the only child of well-to-do parents, his dad a professor of oncology at the university's medical school, Alfred Baumann had been educated K–12 (as they say nowadays but did not then) at private day schools whose graduates routinely matriculated in the Ivy League. At puberty he discovered in himself a passion for the arts and for academic scholarship; decided by his junior prep-school year that he'd be a poet, a professor of literature or maybe of art history, and on the side a jazz pianist, although he knew his way around classical guitar and string bass as well. Enrolled in the comparably prestigious but decidedly less classy VVLU instead of Harvard/Yale/Princeton, because it offered an experimental program wherein selected students could on their adviser's recommendation become virtual Ph.D. candidates early in their undergraduate careers, commence supervised original research in their chosen disciplines, and complete their doctorates as early as five years after matriculation. Al was, moreover, no stranger to the capitals of Europe and elsewhere, the Baumanns having often vacationed abroad before and after the war as well as having gone with Doctor Dad to oncological conferences in sundry foreign venues—whence their son had acquired what to friend Will, at least, was an enviable familiarity with places and languages, wines and cuisines, and the ways of the world, including self-confidence with the opposite sex: a sophistication the more impressive because worn lightly, even self-deprecatingly.

"Trivia," Al liked to say about such casually imparted but attentively received life lessons as that slope-shouldered red-wine bottles contain Burgundies and round-shouldered ones Bordeaux, the former to be enjoyed promptly and the latter "laid down" some years to mature; that both kinds need to "breathe" awhile after opening before being drunk (except for Châteauneuf-du-Pape); that *provolone* has four syllables, not three; that making circles with one's thumbs and forefingers is a handy reminder that one's bread plate on a restaurant table is the one at one's left hand (small "b") and one's drinking glass the one at one's right (small "d"): "It's what's *here, here,* and *here* that matters," indicating in turn his or Will's (or Winnie's) head, heart, and crotch. But from whom if not gentle (slope-shouldered, indeed Chianti-bottle-shaped) Al Baumann did Will learn how to tie a full-Windsor necktie knot, navigate the city's bus and trolley lines, successfully hail a cruising taxicab and compute the driver's tip, play sambas and rhumbas and kazatskies and frailichs as the occasion warranted in addition to their new jazz trio's usual repertory? Not to mention what one learned from him in the classroom, as one's junior instructor in Literature & Philosophy I & II, about Homer and Virgil (and Sappho and Petronius and Catullus), Plato and Aristotle (and the Gnostics and the Kabbalists), Dante and Chaucer and Boccaccio (and Scheherazade and Somadeva, Poggio and Aretino and Rabelais), and other classics on (and off) one's freshman/sophomore syllabus, up to and including James Joyce's *Ulysses* (and *Finnegans Wake*) . . .

"And *trivia,* class, as you may have heard, comes from Latin *trivium:* literally, a place where three roads intersect —as in Sophocles?—but by extension any public square where people swap idle gossip." The Trivium was also (he went on) the medieval division of the seven liberal arts into Grammar, Logic, and Rhetoric—not to be confused with Cambridge University's tripos, which was a different story altogether: "Okay?"

If you say so, Teach. And so indeed Al said, back then back there, in class and out—all which curricular and extracurricular input Will Chase eagerly "downloaded," as one might put it three decades later, his own background having been a different story indeed from Alfred Baumann's: Depression-era child of minimally schooled though by no means unintelligent small-town storekeepers in the state's least affluent county; graduate of a wartime local public school system so strapped for funds and faculty that its eleventh grade was perforce one's senior year, whence nearly none of the seventeen-year-old diplomates "went off" to college—especially if they'd been lucky enough to escape military service and thus unlucky enough to have no GI Bill to subsidize a higher education that, as a group, they weren't competitive for admission to anyhow. A few of the girls managed nursing school, secretarial school, or the nearby teachers college; most became store clerks, telephone operators, beauticians, or/and young housewives and mothers. Most of the boys found jobs in local offices and retail stores or became tradesmen, farmers, or crab-and-oyster watermen like their dads before them. A few enlisted in the peacetime military. And a handful shrug-shoulderedly took the application exam one spring afternoon for "senatorial" scholarships (whereof every Annapolis legislator was allotted a few to award and then to renew or redistribute annually) to various colleges and universities in the Old Line State. Having so done, the applicants proceeded to their summer employment fully expecting that at season's end it would become their *real* employment: their life's work.

Which, however, in Will Chase's case and that of a few others in his (all-white) graduating class, it did not. Since junior high school—or "upper elementary," as sixth and seventh grades were called in that abbreviated system—the lad had made an avid, if noisy, hobby of jazz percussion, and with comparably amateur-but-dedicated classmates on piano, trombone, and alto saxophone had formed a combo to play weekend dances at the local yacht and country club. In the spring of their "senior" year—thanks to the sax-man's father's business connection with a club member who had further connections up and down Maryland's Eastern Shore, they auditioned for and by golly won the best summer job any of them could imagine: At a fading old steamboat-era resort on the upper Chesapeake, still visited in season by daily excursion boats from Baltimore, the quartet would play two hours of dance music in the waterfront dance hall every afternoon while the boat was in and three hours more every evening for vacationers-in-residence, in return for a modest salary and free lodging in a storeroom-turned-bunkhouse at the end of the club's pier. Better yet, on Saturdays the oddly instrumented foursome was to expand to a small orchestra: three saxes (their alto plus two tenors or maybe even a baritone, if they could find one), three brass (the trombonist-leader plus two trumpets, if they could be found), and three rhythm (pianist and drummer plus a bassist, if et cetera). Swing-band-type lighted music stands; uniforms (broad-shouldered lapelless jackets and slightly pegged pants were "hep" just then, also black knit neckties and black-plastic-framed eyeglasses, whether one needed them or not); upgraded (secondhand) Zildjian cymbals and Slingerland drums! Instead of the combo's one-volume fake-book of the melody lines and chord progressions of all the standards, and their improvised "head arrangements" of whatever was current or recent on the Hit Parade, they would have a veritable library of store-bought stock arrangements with separately printed parts for every instrument—plus any "specials" that might be scored by whoever in the group had sufficient interest and ability in the orchestration way.

Which Whoever turned out, if mainly by default, to be Will Chase. Although he'd had no musical training beyond the half-dozen years of piano lessons that most youngsters took in those days, he had learned from them some basics of theory and harmony as well as how to read music, and from his combo-comrades something of the ranges and peculiarities of their instruments. All hands were, moreover, rapt listeners to the exciting new progressive-jazz recordings of Stan Kenton, arranged by Pete Rugolo; to Billy Strayhorn's sophisticated arrangements for Duke Ellington; and to Sy Oliver's for Tommy Dorsey. And so while his buddies expanded and numbered the library, acquired the dressy music stands and the group's first-ever sound system (as primitive by later, rock-era standards as a manual typewriter in the age of desktop computers), and scrambled for the weekend supplement of sidemen and for manageable rehearsal times and venues, Will set about earnestly trying his hand not at composition, for which he knew himself to have no gift, but at transforming by reorchestration some existing, preferably familiar melody into something new, an attention-getting showcase for the band. So enamored of and engrossed in this novel activity of arranging did he become in the spring of that year, and even more so when the expanded orchestra was actually recruited, rehearsed, and swinging on summer Saturday nights at the Bohemia Beach Club, that he dared to imagine—as he never would have about his at-best-adequate instrumental ability—that here might be his vocation: his true calling.

"But it wasn't, quite," Narrator hears the tutelary spirit of Al Baumann interrupt this extended interruption-of-an-interruption to declare, "and so when the Bohemia gig runs its course in late August and our webfoot Wilfred wonders what to do with himself next, he takes his bass player's advice and the scholarship he claims to've forgotten he'd applied for, and he climbs out of his down-county tidemarshes like a wide-eyed, wet-behind-the-ears amphibian and crosses the Bay to join me at VVLU—and there they-all sit at the present time of this so-called story, interrupted by that second phone call, but you've been nattering on so about the Hicksville school system et cet that you haven't even gotten yet to the Three Freds' *ménage à deux et un peu,* and Lou Levy's Cheatery, and why Winnie used to take all our phone calls at Briarwood Three-oh-four. Your Tutelary Spirit suggests you save all this Arranger stuff for a memoir somewhere down the road and get on with our made-up story: Win can't keep Levy on hold forever."

Roger wilco, old buddy—after establishing (a) that this six-hours-a-day, six-days-a-week band gig (Mondays off) taught Will Chase unequivocally that his orchestration, like his percussion, was after all no more than a better-than-average amateur flair, not a pre-professional talent; also (b) that the search for those additional Saturday-night side-men turned up a few college types from Baltimore who commuted to the job by excursion boat and stayed overnight in the club storeroom with the combo—among them the pianist-turned-bassist Alfred Baumann from what we're calling Veritas Vos Liberabit University, that being its motto, and his Goucher College girlfriend Winifred Stark, a Library Science major and Music minor (commuting downtown to her keyboard lessons at the Peabody Institute) every bit as able on piano as was her versatile boyfriend, or for that matter the group's regular ivory-tickler, who therefore happily took weekends off, as the other sidemen could not. And (c), as has been intimated, that it was Will Chase's fortuitous acquaintance with said bassist (the first he'd ever worked with, and what a difference in the band's beat, and how much one learned from him on the job, about everything from leaving the basic four-to-the-bar mainly to him and using one's bass drum more for accents, to pushing one's already-thinning hair into a fifties-style pompadour!) that persuaded him, not to abandon music, but to set aside career ambitions in that line and give college a try instead, at least for his scholarship year. He remains much obliged to this hour, long-gone Al-pal, for that suggestion.

"Well: My suggestion, as you call it, was that after that shall-we-say Bohemian summer, Will Chase would be a fucking idiot to go back to his dear damp Marshville instead of giving big-city academia a try. That he had a better shot at quote Finding Himself, whoever *that* might be, in a VVLU seminar room across the Bay than in his folks' ma-and-pa drugstore. Besides which, Win and I needed a drummer for the new club-style trio that we had in mind but hadn't named yet, and given our three first names, the choice was a no-brainer, as they say nowadays but didn't back then. So introduce us to the Reader already, okay? Something more than that résumé stuff a few pages ago?"

Narrator's pleasure, if Will Chase ever finds his voice. Meet Al Baumann, Reader: twenty-one years old at the time here told of, but already deep into Otto Rank's 1909 treatise *Der Mythus von der Geburt des Helden;* also Lord Raglan's magisterial synthesis *The Hero* (1936), and his own interdisciplinary doctoral dissertation on the Ur-Myth's ubiquity in the literature of Western civilization—

"Not just *Western,* man! And not just the guy's *birth,* either: I was into the whole Heroic Cycle shtick already by the time Campbell's *Hero with a Thousand Faces* came out in 'forty-nine."

That you were—as one appreciates now but could scarcely then. If things had gone differently, it'd be Alfred Baumann instead of Joseph Campbell whom we'd be watching public-television documentaries about.

"So it goes."

So it went, alas, as shall be revealed if Narrator ever gets his act together. Meanwhile, *meet Al Baumann,* Reader: a gentle and wispy-haired but nonetheless commanding presence, lightly brown-goateed a dozen-plus years before the high sixties brought male face hair back into style, and figured not unlike the instrument he played so authoritatively at Will Chase's side on the bandstand of the Bohemia Beach Club and, subsequently, in what passed for a student hangout at super-serious VVLU—a hangout denominated, by that bass-shaped bassist himself, the Trivium . . .

"Because all three curricular roads there met, Reader: the colleges of Arts and Sciences, Engineering, and what's now called Professional Studies but used to be Business and Education."

Plus all three campus castes: undergrads, grad students, and the odd junior instructor or assistant prof.

"Plus our dates, unless we were already-married war vets: the belles of Goucher and dear nearby CONDOM—"

Their sacrilegious acronym, Reader, for the all-female College of Notre Dame of Maryland: doubly titillating to horny VVLUers inasmuch as contraception in that precinct was an even bigger no-no than premarital sex.

"As for one's bearded, bass-shaped bassist-buddy: Granted, I was no skinny-assed redneck like some band-mates I could mention. Ate too much dreck, drank too much National Bohemian, smoked too many of the free cigarettes handed out in our student union by tobacco companies looking to get us hooked, and didn't exercise half enough, despite Doctor Dad's tongue-tsking. But 'twas chiefly a product of inherited metabolism—and anyhow none of the above is known to cause leukemia, which takes care of your why-no-PBS-documentaries question. On to Winnie?"

With pained pleasure, while that so-able and magnanimous rosy-cheeked lass remains freeze-framed back in academic 1948–49, telephone in hand, awaiting the end of this interrupted interruption of Section One, "The Call," of Part One, TELL ME, of our novella-triad *Where Three Roads Meet* . . .

"*Your* novella-triad, man. I just keep the beat."

Nope: Al and Will together kept the beat, with a little

help from Winnie Stark's left hand, while her right both carried our tune and developed and resolved it. Win is the without-whom-not of this Three Freds combo.

"Of their combo, maybe; but their story's *your* baby, excuse the expression. On with it?"

Only children both; pals and playmates since early childhood; their parents near neighbors in upscale-but-laid-back Roland Park, not far from the campuses of their kids' respective day schools and subsequent colleges . . .

"Not that we didn't *consider* Harvard or Princeton and Radcliffe or Smith after finishing Gilman and Bryn Mawr, mind—just as we'd now and then considered other one-and-onlies besides each other. But as has been mentioned, only VVLU was offering that fast-track Ph.D. . . ."

And Goucher was the best nondenominational women's college in the same town, and the girl- and boyfriend competition never measured up to what you K–12 sweethearts—K–sixth form?—had become for each other over the years.

"Reader might as well hear that Win and I were in each other's pants from our let's-play-doctor days through the look-what-I'm-sprouting-down-here and just-got-my-first-period period. Neither of us knows whether I technically deflowered her with my lower-school finger or my upper-school cock, but either way it was at least as much on her initiative as on mine. And we'd been so close already for so long in so many ways that if anything in that line felt *naughty* to us, it was because we were virtual sibs. Which is how your Chianti-bottle buddy managed to score such a doll. Why Win wasn't preggers by age fifteen used to be a mystery to both of us—but I'm getting ahead of your story: Tell."

So *meet Winifred Stark,* Reader: ample-figured, chubby-cheeked, blue-eyed strawberry blondie, her dad a mid-scale real estate developer thriving in the postwar housing boom from which many of the city's now-inner suburbs date; her mom a depressive alcoholic, alas, periodically drying out in nearby Sheppard Pratt Hospital between extended listless, even bedridden stretches at home—a woman driven to drink, as Al's dad diagnosed it, by her failures as a wife and mother because driven to drink—and Al's mom, *faute de mieux,* more a mother to our Win than was her own mother.

"Which benevolent circumstance, needless to add, made us feel more than ever like brother and sister—especially upon that unhappy woman's demise in Winnie's tenth year, whereafter a series of housekeepers attended her pa while Doc and Miz Baumann embraced his daughter as virtually their own."

An upbeat, firm-willed, independent-spirited lass, be it said, who welcomed their monitoring, took the loss of her not-much-of-a-mother in stride, comforted her not-all-that-bereft father as best a third- or fourth-grader can, and threw herself into her schoolwork, music lessons, team sports, and bosom-buddyhood with young Al Baumann. To whom she enjoyed mischievously displaying and even offering to his touch the not-yet-budding bosoms that anon would blossom into adolescent splendor.

"Squeezed and licked into full bloom, we half believed, in our let's-be-naughty sessions in the loft of the Starks' quote Carriage House, as was her playmate's uncircumcised shlong. Not quite your mythic hero's Summons to Adventure, but pretty exciting to us pre-teenies."

Who then as high-schoolers duly dated others, *pour le sport;* groped and were groped by same within modest limits, but always with relief came back from these amusing excursions to each other, with whom by then so much went without saying that they could get on with their joint story without forever having to rebegin it *Once upon a time.*

"And speaking of which—I mean getting on with one's story . . . ?"

On with same they got: Went off to their respective college freshman years at campuses less than five miles apart. Promised their respective parents (Win had a stepmom by then, whom, contrary to stereotype, she liked better than she'd ever liked her late mother) that they'd not marry until they'd completed their degrees, nor "live together" in the meanwhile—that being a thing still Not Done, by and large, among people of their sort in those days, although the aforenoted presence on campus of so many married war vets was loosening the old conventions. Dwelt therefore in their respective college dorms for that first year, they did, it being agreed by all hands that Getting Out of the House was a significant part of one's higher education, and then in just-off-campus apartments with same-sex roommates through their second year—each often "sleeping over" in the other's flat. In that year too their growing interest in jazz, especially of the Progressive and then the Cool varieties (an interest that Narrator ought to've re-established two pages ago, but neglected to), led them to exchange their extracurricular hobby of playing chamber music with Win's Peabody pals for working dance gigs with a local non-union outfit.

"Because as scabs we earned less per job than the union guys in town, but scored more jobs."

While at the same time, in young Baumann's case, so impressing his VVLU Humanities profs and adviser that by the end of his second college year (one can't, strictly speaking, say "sophomore year," inasmuch as in the university's fast-track advanced-degree program he was already a "pre-doc," neither an undergraduate nor quite a graduate student) he was invited to enroll in graduate-level seminars the following year and perhaps to be a junior instructor in his department's two-year undergrad survey course called Literature & Philosophy.

"By which was meant representative classics of both disciplines in Western Civ, Reader, from Homer and the pre-Socratics up to maybe Nietzsche and Dostoyevsky, and their arguably reciprocal influence: one major weekly lecture to the whole class by appropriate bigshots on the senior faculty, followed by twice-weekly small-section follow-ups led by us JIs. No better way to study that high-protein stuff than to have to teach it."

And teach it he did, young Alfred B., to the lucky dozen or so freshmen who happened to draw his section. The particular blank tablet named Wilfred Chase learned more from him in two semesters than he'd learned in two years at Back-Home High—and not just about Lit & Phil, nor only in class.

"W.C.'s *tabula* wasn't all that *rasa,* man—but you're ahead of our story, no?"

Not really, once Reader is reminded that between Al's and Winnie's second and third college years came that Bohemia Beach Club summer afore-rehearsed, their attendant connection with and befriendment of Adequate Drummer and Strictly Amateur Arranger Wilfred Chase, their persuading him to give college a try despite his less than impressive academic preparation therefor, and their case-clinching invitation to him to be the third Fred in the light-jazz trio they had in mind to play weekend gigs in the new student hangout that they were trying to get renamed the Trivium. All of which came to pass.

"And more."

More indeed—such as Will's barely hanging on, academically, through the overwhelmment of that freshman year. Democritus and Lucretius to Hume and Schopenhauer! Euripides and Plautus to Goethe and Molière! Renaissance, Reformation and Counter Reformation! Neoclassics and Romantics! Who knew?

"Well . . ."

Patient and bemused A. Baumann did, for one, and lively-friendly W. Stark, who were living together by then in Briarwood 304, but who for the sake of appearances listed that Murphy-bedded studio apartment as hers alone and the one below it, 204, as his and his same-sex roommate's: posh accommodation indeed for a webfoot redneck greenhorn out of his depth!

"Out of his depth, maybe, but paddling madly and not quite sinking after all, while downloading not only old Lit-Phil One and Two, and Burgundies versus Bordeaux—"

And trolley cars and taxicabs! Lacrosse and tennis and chess! Frat-house binges and East Baltimore Street burlesque! Also classmates Jewish and Catholic, Asian and Indian, European and Canadian and Latin American—

"But not yet *African* American, shame to say, in those still-segregated days. And our Wilfred downloaded not only these exotic marvels, one was saying . . ."

But also a much-improved acquaintance with the non-academic world of work—especially after his unimpressive freshman-year grade point average cost him his scholarship. With the best will in the world, excuse the poor pun, Chase *père* and *mère* could manage no more than half his VVLU tuition, they having aged parents to help provide for and their own elder years a-coming. The other half, plus room and board and books and spending money, their son had to scramble for, he being by then determined to hang on in that venue at whatever cost, to the end not only of imbibing more Lit & Phil—

"Not to mention History, Economics, Sciences both Natural and Social, a second language or two, and a few other items—"

But also in hopes of discovering the True Vocation that music had turned out not to be, nor scholarship either, QED: a calling more specific than the "Humanities" he'd chosen as his *faute de mieux* freshman-year major. In short, learning who and what he was and deciding who and what to be, in the way Al Baumann *knew* himself to be a Lit-Phil professor-in-the-works, and Winnie Stark *knew* she was some sort of librarian-to-be and Al's lifelong soulmate. That pair being, as afore-observed, the sole offspring of better-heeled families, their Three Freds dance gigs earned them spending money over and above their parents' generous provision and Al's junior-instructor stipend. Will, on the other hand, while still beat-keeping for the Freds on weekends, worked another job and a half that summer to support himself and make tuition payments: as a full-time night-shift timekeeper at a steel mill on the city's east side, and by day as a part-time roach-spray salesman in its bug-infested black ghettos, among sundry other pickup employments, all of which enriched his résumé of extracurricular real-world experience beyond high school clerking in his parents' store and musicianing in the (by-then-defunct) Bohemia Beach Club.

"And taught him, by the way, that the worlds of white-collar office work and product-peddling, like those of store-clerking and the blue-collar trades, were not for him, except as stopgaps. While to the more appealing calls of music and scholarship he found himself no more capable of professional-level response than to that of tennis, say, or chess. But tell me, man: Is this the Three Freds Story, or the one about How Will Chase Found His Voice?"

Those stories are one story, to which can now be added (what Reader may well have surmised) that for whatever mix of reasons—simple generosity and hospitality, amused fascination with a rustic innocent, reluctance to find and break in a brand-new replacement drummer if the incumbent flunked—

"All of the above, plus one thing more—"

Freds One and Two, who had befriended their country cousin on the Bohemia Beach bandstand and coached him (Al especially, but not exclusively) through his freshman-year survival struggles, had by that year's end virtually adopted him. Not as a son, mind, the kid they'd never have . . .

"Ouch."

Sorry there. But more as a not-unpromising but thitherto deprived kid brother, to be gently initiated into assorted mysteries large and small.

"Not unpromising indeed. The fact is, Reader, that just as Will Chase's first Great Ambition had been music, for which alas he simply hadn't the right stuff or anyhow enough thereof, so Fred One, as I seem to be being designated, had since boyhood more than anything aspired, not to *teach* Lit and Phil, honorable as that profession is, but to *create* same—especially the former. For which however alas et cetera? Granted, he might discern precociously the outlines of the Ur-Myth, say, and in order to trace its ubiquity in the literatures of the world he might take unto himself the vast corpus of those literatures, insofar as a brash twenty-one-year-old insomniac can—"

Which is to say, pretty fucking far.

"But he would eagerly have swapped all that for the gift of adding even a single small item to the inventory: not a learned commentary, but a capital-T Text! Not one more *midrash,* but a bit o' Scripture! In that line, however, as in at least one other . . ."

Never mind, please. Sufficient to say that said Fred now saw fit to see in his Bohemia gig-mate, later his eagerest student and then his protégé and official-though-not-actual apartment-mate—and moreover to persuade Fred Two that *she* saw as well—what said gig-mate/student/et cetera would scarcely have presumed to see in himself: the potential for doing, artfully, what his benevolent mentor had so aspired to.

"Which artfulness, shall we call it, extends to Narrator's keeping Our Winifred, shall we call her, on hold, let's say, for lo these many pages, phone in hand on hand-me-down couch in Briarwood Three-zero-four with Lou Levy on the line, the Triple-F story's Present Action frozen in interrupted mid-interruption while he takes his sweet time and ours filling in the blanks of Background. Far be it from a mere bass-shaped scholar-critic to criticize, but one wonders whether Narrator's artfulness mightn't extend further to wrapping up this extended Exposition and *getting on with the effing story,* at least Part One thereof, dot dot dot question mark? *Tell Me,* man!"

Roger maybeco, old buddy who never had the much-mixed blessing of growing old. The Effing Story is what's getting itself told, believe it or not, in its less-than-straightforward fashion: a story one of whose apparent meanders fetched us to that spring '49 mid-morning in Briarwood 304 when nineteen-year-old Wilfred Chase, winding up his sophomore year at VVLU and hearing once again his mentor-friend's trademark imperative *Tell Me,* set about happily reminding all hands of that so-consequential mid-term day in Alfred Baumann's freshman Lit & Phil section when the young instructor had drawn on the blackboard an equiangular Y and said, "Okay, guys: In eight to ten pages' worth of sentences both articulate and legible, tell me before next Friday what this symbol says to you." Which recounting —prompted by Winnie Stark's observation that her gynecologist's wall chart of the Human Female Reproductive System (by her remarked on her recent annual visit to that office), with its bubblegum-pink fallopian tubes converging L & R upon the uterine cervix, was yet another pregnant analogue, so to speak, to the Place Where Three Roads Meet—had been interrupted and remained suspended by what we would learn presently but did not yet know just then to be a phone call from Louis Levy: proprietor, headmaster, and sole full-time employee of the Levy Preparatory School, a.k.a. the Cheatery.

The Important Thing, Will had been saying back then, was not that he'd happened in that mid-term essay to mention a number of associations that his so-savvy instructor hadn't thought of, like say the confluence of sperm and egg into embryo, or for that matter of father and mother into child—or, in the other direction, the forking of headwaters into river branches or tree trunks ditto, echoing the Primordial One's self-division, in sundry myths already mentioned in class, into Two and thence into Many; or (reversing Al's analogue of Hegelian dialectic, wherein Thesis versus Antithesis gives rise to Synthesis) the anti-Synthetic process of Analysis . . .

"What I *had* mentioned," put in Al here (back there back then, for Winnie's benefit), "—along with Siamese twins sharing a single lower body, like the mythical Meliónides who fought Herakles, and the actual freaks illustrated in Aldrovandi's sixteenth-century *Monstrorum Historia*—was how at the Deutsches Eck in Koblenz, where the green Moselle joins the mud-brown Rhine, one is reminded not only of Hegelian Synthesis but of why Moselle wines come in green bottles and Rhine wines in brown. What F-Three added was that his Chesapeake tidal rivers, like say the handsome Wye (but *un*like its eponymous one-way English counterpart), switch from Synthesis to Analysis, or Fusion to Diffusion, every six and a half hours, changing the Place Where Three Roads Meet, or two become one, into the place where one becomes two. But that's not what mattered."

Yes it isn't. What mattered, as Will was saying to Al and Win (not for the first time) when the phone rang (ditto), was that he'd seen fit to cast these mid-term observations, whatever their merits, into the form of a gloss on Robert Frost's poem "The Road Not Taken" ("Two roads diverged in a yellow wood," et cetera), which the Lit & Phillers had read earlier that semester: more specifically, into the first-person monologue of a nonconformist spermatozoon swimming alone against the current up a different fork of some dark stream from the one that his countless ejaculation-mates have chosen, and speculating on the overall layout of wherever in the world he is and on the mystery of what it's all about . . .

"Poor shmuck," had commiserated Winnie—who, like Al but not yet like Will, had acquired a handy array of Yiddish disparagements from Jewish friends and classmates.

"Poor *fucking* shmuck," had added Al: From the veterans on campus all hands were picking up the liberal use of what they called "the word that won the war."

Yes, well. What mattered, Narrator had been gratefully reminding them when the telephone rang, was that upon reading said mid-term essay its author's instructor was even more pleased by the narrative conceit and prose style than by what it had to say about that equiangular Y: enough so that he not only A-plused it but declared to the Three Freds' drummer at their next Trivium session, "What we have on our hands here, my friend, is a capital-G fucking Gift: the one you wished you'd had for music but did not, and the one I wish *I* had for lit-making but do not. We're talking capital-V Vocation, man! The capital-C fucking mythic-heroical Call!"

Of the authenticity whereof he became so generously convinced—through the rest of that freshman semester and the next, and the summer following and the sophomore fall semester after that, as the Three Freds worked, played, and, increasingly, lived together—that at his urging, self-skeptical Will gave VVLU's Rudiments of Narrative course a try. And although he learned more from his mentor-friend's editorial comments on those primitive efforts (and from keen-eared Winnie's, and from the classic authors they bade him read) than from his classmates and course instructor, Fred-the-Mentee resolved, in the semester following (i.e., spring '49, the "now" of this section of this Three Freds story), to change his academic major from General Arts and Sciences to the university's recently established program in Creative Writing: not necessarily what Al Baumann thought the best curriculum for aspiring writers, inasmuch as literature had managed quite well for millennia without such programs, but he shrugged his (non-)shoulders at the news and agreed that further intensive practice, with feedback more various than his and Winnie's alone, wouldn't likely do harm and might well be of some benefit—*if* one were sufficiently alive to Literature's vastness and variety to counter every facile generalization about what constitutes Good Writing with an inarguably brilliant contradictory example.

This would by him get said, of course, only after Will got *his* say said: his declaration of major-changing intent, with which he meant to follow his grateful reminiscence-in-progress of that first-semester term paper on Analogues to the Y which had led him to what he was now entirely persuaded was his true Calling, however ably or otherwise he responded to that call. And it was in the midst of just that reminiscence that Briarwood 304's telephone rang, first with a wrong number and then—as Will was saying "As I was saying, guys"—with a mellifluous baritone response to Winifred Stark's "Hello?"

"Is there a Wilfred Chase there, please? Louis Levy calling."

Win arched her never-plucked eyebrows, puckered her ever-unpainted lips, beamed conspiratorially at Freds One and Three, held out the receiver to that latter, silently mouthed the name *Lou Levy,* and (not for the first or last time in this trio's history) said to same, "It's yours."

2. THE CHEATERY

In his Lit & Phil class discussions of Truth, Goodness, and Beauty, Alfred Baumann was at pains to distinguish Truth from Fact: "We speak of the truths of great novels, or the truths of great myths, even though both involve made-up stories," et cetera. And he was fond of pointing out to his students how different were the meanings of *Veritas vos liberabit* to Jesus, for example (as quoted by his disciple John in the eponymous book, 8:32); to the research university whose motto, eighteen centuries later, those words became; and to the newly founded U.S. Central Intelligence Agency, which had also seen fit to appropriate that "bit o' Scripture" as its motto. He enjoyed pointing out (the class was reading Sophocles) that while "the truth" might indeed be liberating—whether from soul-damning Error in the first instance, intellectual benightedness in the second, or perilous ignorance of what the nation's designated enemies were up to in the third—it could also be devastating, even fatal, as witness poor Oedipus and various other tragic heroes. "*Gnothi seauton,* the Delphic oracle advises," he would remind his more or less attentive freshmen. "*Know thyself.* Because, adds Socrates, *the unexamined life is not worth living.* So, then: Was Oedipus in better shape, was he more quote-unquote *free,* for learning that the old guy he'd knocked off at the Place Where Three Roads Meet was in fact his dad, who'd tried and failed to have *him* knocked off at birth? And that the widow-queen he'd then married and sired kids upon was his birth-mom? Remembering the King James Bible sense of 'to know' as 'to have carnal knowledge of,' one could fairly say that in Oedipus's case, to know himself was to screw himself altogether! So tell me: Given that for him the *examined* life was literally unlivable, would our Oed have been better off *not* knowing? One bluebook's or fifty minutes' worth of lucid commentary, s.v.p., whichever comes first."

Although never a varsity athlete, senior class officer, or other sort of high school bigshot, Wilfred Chase (wrestling determinedly there in the third row with Al's bluebook question) had been a not-unpopular teenager who'd quite enjoyed his small-town adolescence despite wartime deprivations and the county's junior-year senior year. He'd been a columnist for the school newspaper and had co-managed the boys' varsity basketball team, had co-organized that aforementioned rudimentary jazz combo, and had dated two or three girls over that foreshortened period. No extended romances, but when his buddies compared notes on their post-prom exploits—typically a matter of who among them had managed, in the lingo of the time, to get to First or even to Second Base with his date—Will was not obliged either to lie or to remain silent at risk of being thought prudish or queer. Few of their age and kind back then could claim honestly to have reached *Third* Base (reciprocal manual masturbation, fellatio, or cunnilingus, for all which they knew only the vulgar terminology); and the few who not only had attained that much-coveted station but had actually "scored" were not inclined to boast of having done so, their partners typically being longtime sweethearts whom they meant to marry "when the time came," and of whose reputations they were therefore, for the most part, honorably protective. He had, had our Will, by his seventeenth birthday French-kissed Vicki Parker as the pair rocked on her front-porch glider; had playfully patted Helen Davis's behind several times while jitterbugging in her family's rec room and teasingly squeezed same while slow-dancing; had fondled Doris Travers's starboard breast through sweater and bra in Schine's Avalon Theatre during a Saturday matinee of *Lady on a Train,* starring Deanna Durbin and Ralph Bellamy; and had done both of the above plus actually getting hand *under* bra (Vicki again, junior/senior prom night, in back seat of Donnie McDougal's parents' brand-new DeSoto) and even *up under skirt and panties,* briefly, where he'd touched the pert blond's presumably-also-blond pubic fur (what did *he* know?), but had been by her firmly escorted off those premises before reaching its sacred precinct, moist heart of the mystery. Into penile masturbation he had been initiated in Boy Scout Camp at age almost-thirteen by pretending that he knew all about it already while an older Eagle Scout in his cabin explained the procedure to a wide-eyed fellow Tenderfoot; thereafter he availed himself of that solitary pleasure with a frequency that he assumed—correctly, as it happens—to be within normal parameters.

That-all said, however, Will himself readily acknowledged to his Fred-friends that as of his matriculation at VVLU, his innocence, of which he was more than ready to be divested, was of an extent whereof he'd been innocently ignorant, excuse all those *of*s: It included not merely the difference between, e.g., Cabernet and Beaujolais, Hapsburg and Hohenzollern, Windsor and four-in-hand, but also—unusual though by no means rare for late-teen small-town middle-class WASP males in those days, unless they were in the military—the ins and outs, so to speak, of intercourse, in both senses, with the opposite sex. Except for Donnie McDougal's older sister Karen—who'd walked bare-ass naked one moonlit July night through her brother's bedroom en route to the house's single toilet while wide-awake Will was sleeping over, and then en route back, as if suspecting that the boys might be only feigning sleep, had paused at their bed-foot and given her plump backside a mischievous twitch or two in their direction before returning to her own bedroom and closing the door—he had never seen a woman in the altogether.

"Whereas Freds One and Two, on the other hand, dot dot dot . . ."

Had been so intimately familiar through so many years

and developmental stages that by the time they reached their twenties and commenced their unofficial cohabitation in Briarwood 304, while not at all bored with each other, they found it erotically interesting, shall we say, to admit the so-innocent Fred Three, gradually, into their intimacy.

"Erotically interesting, yes: We *shall* say that. Part of his tutelage in Truth, Goodness, and Beauty, though more to do with life's facts than with its capital-T Truths."

Thus did it amuse and perhaps mildly titillate Will's teacher-pal to emerge grinning one January late afternoon from 304's bathroom (whereto he'd excused himself to take a leak while the threesome were playing hearts) brandishing Winnie's douche syringe, with its large red rubber squeeze-bulb and its penis-length curved black plastic nozzle, and to declare, "Pop-quiz time, Wilfredo: What is this instrument, and to what end, so to speak, is it applied?" And then—when the best his protégé could come up with (pretty sure he was mistaken) was "Enema?"—merrily demanded of eye-rolling Winifred that she enlighten their benighted combo-colleague, "with or without demonstration, as your pedagogical sense inclines." And enlighten him she did, plucky girl: In the I'll-show-*you* spirit of mock-indignant retaliation that she and Al not infrequently assumed for their own entertainment, she plunked down her cards, snatched the item from him, bade him sit and not *dare* peek while she led their much-discomfited tutee into the bathroom, closed the door halfway, and in a voice pitched to carry through the apartment, said, "So let's pretend that that charming chap and I have just *fucked,* okay? And even though his charming little pecker may be less formidable than this charming dildo here, it will have managed to unload a charming troop of little Al Baumanns into you-know-where. Or maybe you *don't* know where, right? So let me just step out of these step-ins and show you. *Now,* then: Our objective being for him and me to have our premarital fun without knocking up poor Winnie before we're official, either our bass player uses a rubber—but what fun is *that?*—or else our post-coital pianist fills this bulb with a spermicidal douche (from the French for 'shower,' mind, not the French for 'sweet,' and plain water will do for this demo). Lacking a proper *bidet Français*—did you know that *un bidet* means an old nag or a trestle as well as a certain hygienic fixture?—she then bestrideth this Yankee toilet like *so,* opens her pearly white thighs like *so,* and—watch closely, now, *enfant* . . . In fact, you can do this part yourself: Be my guest, and gently, please, in and out, *au point d'orgasm. Entendu?*"

Et cetera, not actually removing her underpants and sitting, much less permitting her awed attendant to insert the nozzle, but giving Al every reason, so it seemed to Will, to imagine otherwise. Grinning broadly, "So, *dites-moi,*" that friend demanded of him when wondering student and triumphant teacher-demonstrator returned to the living room, "d'j'ever see such a pettable puss? But don't forget"—holding up a warning forefinger—"I'm the only one who *really* gets to see it, not to mention—*hey!*" For here the faux-indignant Winnie picked up her wineglass from the card table and dumped several ounces of Sauvignon Blanc onto her lover's head. Laughing with him then while still standing between the seated males, "I'll show *you,* Mister Wiseass!" she said, and yanked her panties down to her knees, then lifted her skirt front with one hand, seized hapless Will by the pompadour with the other, and in fact showed *him,* nose to bush, the dainty precinct under discussion. "Truth, Goodness, and Beauty: *voilà!*"

"All in one piece," wowed Wilfred managed to marvel, and for that *double-entendre bon mot* got his face pressed briefly but squarely into it. Lesson done then, Win pulled up her underpants, and the laughing trio resumed their card game. Reraising his forefinger, "Fifty years down the road," Al predicted—not altogether in jest, so it seemed to Will—"some academic hack like me will do a doctoral dissertation called *Briarwood 304: The Moral/Aesthetic/Erotic Initiation of Wilfred Chase.*"

"*Or,*" added Winnie, sorting her cards, "*The Post-Joycean Novelist as Quasi-Mythic Wandering Hero.* Dissertation subtitles have to have an *as.*"

"You're no academic hack," loyally protested Will. "And I'm no Post-Joycean Quasi-Mythic Wandering Whatever."

"Not yet, for damn sure," his mentor agreed, then resumed his mock-solemn air: "But mark my words, comrades: Half a century down the road, this three-way-hearts-game afternoon when Stark first rubbed Chase's nose in Truth Goodness and Beauty will be seen to have been a literary-historical turning point. The Ur-Mythic Summons to Adventure! The fucking *Call!*"

Offered somewhat flustered though deeply flattered Will, "Another archetypal Y? The Stark Pudendum as Nowise-Trivial Trivium? But I forgot to notice whether it's equiangular."

"I'll let you know in the morning," Al promised. "Unless Win wants to continue your French lesson now?"

"Kiss my sweet *as,*" growled she, "the pair of you. And let's *play,* okay?"

Play they did (after Al informed them that the above-alluded-to Irish Modernist émigré writer, responding to a critic's charge that the language-play of *Finnegans Wake* was "ultimately trivial," had declared, "I'm not trivial; I'm *quadrivial*"): played through that academic year, and not only at their card games, their verbal badinage, and their jazz sessions at the Trivium (where, they agreed, long musical comradeship had given them a nonverbal, nondiscursive, but subtle and eloquent medium of three-way communication rich in cues, signals, teasing or serious queries and responses, improvised joint statements, and trial-and-error experiments), but with Truth, Goodness, and Beauty as well.

Know thyself . . . At this point in his story, what Will Chase understood of himself included that he was physically okay: tall, lean, healthy, free of disfigurement, and, though not particularly handsome, not physiognomically ill-favored either. Historically fortunate, too, having been born to comfortably middle-class American parents in just the right historical "window" to miss both world wars (not here for the first, too young to serve in the second) and to be scarcely aware of the Great Depression of the 1930s, which his parents had gamely scrimped through in their son's grade school years. That although no whiz kid like Al and Winnie, he was reasonably intelligent. Not well educated by their enviable standard, but learning fast and eagerly. Not remarkably brave, he supposed (never having been put to serious test in that department), but no coward either, he'd bet. No longer a believer in God (he had shrugged off in high school his parents' perfunctory Protestantism), but withal a morally inclined and ethically decent fellow by his own estimation despite some questionable, mainly experimental lapses, to be reviewed shortly. And finally, that in place of the professional-caliber musical talent that he had erst so craved but was reconciled to lacking, he had been endowed with (or was anyhow resolved to acquire and develop) a Way with Words.

As to those Mainly Experimental Lapses: "Intense, even impassioned moral/ethical *concern,*" Alfred Baumann would remind his students when they were reading Plato and Dostoyevsky, "doth not in itself a moral person make." What ardent discussions he and his Lit & Phillers enjoyed, in class and in Briarwood 304, about Raskolnikov and Svidrigailov, about the mischievously appealing *Symposium*-crasher Alcibiades, about the atomic bombings of Hiroshima and Nagasaki . . . Yet (or *And*) in the same spirit wherewith Will especially, as the least experienced of the Freds, calibrated his tolerance for alcohol by exceeding it, and the threesome shared occasional "reefers" back when few of their age and station had ever seen marijuana, much less used it, they found it mildly exciting—and not morally indefensible, they half-seriously opined, for low-budget students in a corporate-capitalist society—to shoplift groceries, say, from large chain supermarkets (though never, they piously agreed, from small independent merchants); to gain sales access to those potential black-ghetto insecticide customers by declaring, "We're the people who've been sent to spray your house," and then, once inside, pitching their product after spraying one room (a single week of this bait-and-switch scam sufficed to turn their moral stomachs; their ever more adventurous shoplifting, however, extended through a full semester and then some, before one of them—Winnie, most likely—asked, "What *are* we, guys, lunatics or hypocritical common thieves?" Whereupon they acknowledged their makeshift rationalizing and forswore further larceny, but made no attempt at restitution); and to misrepresent to the Baumann/Stark parents, "for their own peace of mind," Al and Winnie's Briarwood cohabitation.

"In short, Reader, we three played with dynamite the way macho schoolboys used to play with lighted firecrackers, seeing who'd hold on longest before tossing them away or losing a finger. And speaking of holding: Has Lou Levy been on hold back there in B Three-oh-four right through this Extended Narrative Digression? Did we even *have* telephonic holds in 'forty-nine?"

Not a digression, really, but an aside on the subject of self-knowledge acquired via Mainly Experimental Detours from what the trio knew very well to be the Straight and Narrow. *Thou shalt not lie,* we learned—about why thou'rt knocking on rowhouse doors, for example, with cockroach-spraygun at the ready. *Nor shalt thou steal*—not even packaged sliced bacon from the A & P . . .

"Win scored a six-pound turkey breast once, remember? Pretending she was preggers!"

And actually got away with that apt-though-painful-in-retrospect foreshadowing: our last major heist before both conscience and commonsense risk-benefit analysis set in.

"And *Thou shalt not cheat*—not even under the benignant cover of Louis Levy's *soi-disant* Preparatory School."

The Cheatery. It has been made clear, Narrator trusts, that the telephone in B 204, "Will's" studio apartment, was listed as Al's, and the one in Al and Winnie's 304 as hers, for reasons of decorum. When therefore Headmaster Levy desired to telephone prospective tutor Wilfred Chase, he rang up the number supplied him by former tutor Alfred Baumann as his own, understanding the pair to be roommates—which number, however, was the one where Al could be reached in fact: B 304's, routinely answered by Winnie. (Dr. and Mrs. Baumann, when phoning their son, soon learned to expect that it would be Wilfred, his official roomie, who took the call and promised to have said son call back "as soon as he comes in." The actual living arrangement must surely have soon been apparent to them, but for decorum's sake they went along with the fiction, as did M/M Stark—and refrained from visiting their children *in situ*, where the charade would have been immediately obvious.) All which explaineth why—when Will took the instrument from Win and said "Hello," and was asked resonantly "Is this Wilfred Chase?" and, instead of acknowledging that he sometimes asked himself the same question, said merely "Speaking"—the hearty reply was "Glad to catch you at home, Mr. Chase! I'm Louis Levy. Perhaps you've heard of me from Al Baumann?"

"I have, sir." To put it mildly.

"One of our best preceptors ever! We were sorry to lose him to the higher realms of academia, but so it goes! Now we're looking for another grad student of his caliber to fill a part-time preceptorship that just opened up here, and Alfred tells me you're our man!"

"Very kind of him," Will allowed, thinking, *Preceptors? Preceptorship? He really calls them that?* Not to mention, *Grad student? Me? Of Al's caliber?*

"You'll be tutoring a handful of high-schoolers in literature and composition, helping them with their essays and other homework assignments. Good kids, some from our private schools and some from the better public ones. Couple of hours every weekday afternoon—say, half past three to half past five? Two bucks an hour. What do you think?"

From across the room Pal Al smiled, as does his ghost when Narrator here recounts this benign surprise, this little joke of a setup. For in Will's scrabbling after part-time work to supplement the Three Freds' weekend wages from the Trivium—the same scrabbling that led him to peddling roach spray, tallying steel-mill timecards, reshelving library books, and various other jobs—he had envied Al the easy two dollars an hour (not bad money in those days) picked up on the side at Lou Levy's establishment one previous semester. "Best way to learn a book or a language is to teach it" was an oft-repeated Baumann article of faith, and while they'd shaken their collective heads at the nature of Levy's downtown-rowhouse "preparatory school" (dedicated mostly to doing rich kids' homework for them, Al had reported), he had found it possible to improve a bit not only the students' reading and writing skills in their native language, but his own appreciation of the poems and essays involved in their homework assignments. And without mentioning the matter to Will, he had recommended him to Levy as his replacement. "Lit and Phil One and Two it ain't," he would say after the phone conversation in progress. "But some of the brats are likable and even teachable, and some of their *preceptors* learn a bit about teaching and about the texts. So give it a shot: one more item in your résumé."

But to his caller Will confessed, "I'm not quite a graduate student, Mr. Levy. Actually, I'm just finishing my sophomore year." And would demand afterward of Al, "Why'd you tell him I was a grad student?"

Replied the mellifluous former with a knowing chuckle, "We quite understand that those distinctions get blurred in your university's new fast-track program. But okay by Al Baumann is okay by us." And the latter, with shrug of hands and eyebrows, "Graduate shmaduate: You're good enough for Levy's Prep, and you'll learn a thing or two. He needs to be able to tell the parents that their heirs are getting individual attention from VVLU grad students—which in effect they are, 'cause I'll be checking on you through the first week and as needed thereafter."

"I'll buy that," Winnie declared at this point—Will having accepted Levy's invitation to hop the bus down St. Paul Street next day for the mere formality of an interview. "Come to think of it, maybe I'll apply for a PTP myself: Part-Time Preceptorship? For *my* résumé."

Which she did, cutting half a day's senior-year classes at Goucher on a pleasant mid-April morning to ride the bus with Fred Three down past the marble-stepped, brick- and Formstone-fronted rowhouse corridor to Levy Prep, and introducing herself to that establishment's pudgy, black-curled, florid-faced, dark-suited but bright-necktied proprietor-cum-headmaster as "Al Baumann's part-time grad-student fiancée—in case you need another preceptor in Literature, History, French, German, or Spanish?"

Replied the amused, unruffled Levy, "Two questions," and raised first his left forefinger: "Are you out to snatch this young man's job before I've even interviewed him?" Then the finger beside it: "And are you a part-time graduate student or Mr. Baumann's part-time fiancée?"

To Will's considerable surprise, as he'd never heard his Fred-friends speak of themselves as officially engaged to marry, she linked her arm with his, gave the two men an exaggerated vampish wink, and said, "*No* to the first and *yes* to the second and third of your two questions." Holding up her own left forefinger, "Al and I think of Wilfred as part of us, and you can't steal from yourself, right?" Then a second finger: "And my courses at Goucher and Peabody this year would be graduate courses if they had a graduate program—which they don't, quite, yet." And then a third: "Plus, Al and I don't regard *affiancement* as a full-time job."

"Lucky fellow," Levy said smoothly to Will, raising his massive eyebrows, stroking his chin, and gesturing us into his office-cum-classroom. To Winnie then (whose arm and Will's were still linked), "And when you say, quote, *which they don't* comma *quite* comma *yet,* unquote, do you mean that they don't have graduate programs quite yet, or that their present programs are as yet not quite graduate programs? Come in, please, and have a seat."

Unhesitatingly, "I quite agree that those propositions are quite different," Win responded. "Excuse the intensifying adverbs? But in this instance, both are quite true." Pointing then to a short list of long words on the blackboard behind the desk labeled HEADMASTER, "I also happen to know what every one of those sesquipedalia means," she declared. "And I'm sure Will does, too: He's the family wordsmith."

With a knowing smile at the papers he was moving about on his desktop, "All in the family, eh?" said Levy. "Now, then, Miss Stark: If you'll just step into the next room for a few minutes, your friend and I will get down to business. After which, maybe you and I can have a little chat."

Sesquipedalian was, in fact, one of the listed words, along with *adjudicatory, misogynistic, eleemosynary,* and our language's longest, *antidisestablishmentarianism.*

"Quite a gal," Levy remarked when Winnie closed the office door behind her. To cover his discomfort at the small smirk in the man's voice and manner, "Smart as a whip," Will agreed, "and plays fine jazz piano as well as classical. She and Al and I work weekends at the VVLU Trivium: piano, bass, and drums. Do you happen to know why people say 'Smart as a whip'?"

For the first time, Levy regarded him with what seemed genuine interest. "I don't, in fact. So tell me, Mister Wordsmith, why do we?"

"Beats me," Will admitted. "And I confess I don't know *eleemosynary,* either."

Turning up his palms, "So look it up!" Levy said. Confidingly then, with a nod at the board behind him, "We teach the kids a few fancy words to impress their teachers with, if they can work 'em into their papers." He stroked his chin. "You're hired, by the way. I see from your transcript," which, per Al's advice, Will had brought a copy of to the interview, "that you got off to a *very* rough start up there and then really hit your stride. That sets the right example for your tutees."

Will reminded him that he wasn't "quote *quite* a graduate student quote *quite yet.*"

"Nor are we quite a preparatory school, strictly speaking." Complicitous smile. "More remedial, actually, though we really do *prepare* the kids' homework assignments. You'll do just fine. Starting tomorrow? And tell your *winsome* friend Miss Chutzpah that we might just have something for her, too, before the school term ends."

As the Freds made dinner *à trois* that evening back in Briarwood 304's tiny kitchenette, "*Winsome,*" Al Baumann echoed, wincing, when that friend reported to him what their friend had reported to her of this conversation: "Our winsome Winnie."

"As in 'You win some and you lose some'" supposed the family wordsmith. "Anyhow, I learned a useful new word today: not *winsome.*"

"*Eleemosynary,* I'll bet," Al teased. "I should've prepped you: Levy had that same list on his blackboard when he interviewed me last year."

Replied Will, "Fuck eleemosynary. On the bus ride home, your *fiancée* Miss Winsome preceptored me in *chutzpah.* We didn't hear much Yiddish back in Marshville."

"*Part-time* fiancée," Win reminded him, and perhaps reminded Al as well, for to Will's considerable surprise—after declaring that although she had indeed explained to him Levy's term for her, Fred Three remained in her estimation lamentably innocent of the quality thereby named—she turned from the stove, embraced that fellow from behind as he chopped onions at the sink, pressed her breasts firmly into his back, reached one hand around to cup his crotch, and declared her conviction that with just a dash of *chutzpah* their drummer-boy could be "a real stud instead of a sexual *ree*-tard." Regarding the pair benignly sidewise from the cutting board on which he was dicing Idaho potatoes, "Maybe the kid needs a part-time preceptor," Al ventured.

"Could be," she agreed. And giving her handful a playful squeeze and pat, she returned to her liver-and-bacon sauté-in-progress.

"Remedial or preparatory?" her prospective tutee pretended to wonder, and in the spirit of their three-way tease, made bold to squeeze in turn one plump-but-firm, beskirted Winnie-buttock. "And when's my first lesson, Teach?"

"Enough *chutzpah* already," declared her part-time fiancé. "Let's fry this stuff and feed our fucking faces."

They did that, bantering of other matters than the one now uppermost in Wilfred Chase's much-aroused narrative imagination; then withdrew to their separate quarters to prepare the next day's schoolwork.

Which in Will Chase's case included not only VVLU's Rudiments of Narrative course—in which he was endeavoring, without impressive success, to "find his own voice" amid the cacophony of his similarly struggling fellow novices and their innumerable full-throated predecessors—

but also his maiden sessions on the other side of the pedagogical divide, "tutoring" Lou Levy's after-school enrollees in what was labeled, simply, English.

"How do I Part-Time Preceptor them?" he had wondered to his own preceptor-in-chief. "What part-time precepts do I have to offer?"

"All of our precepts are part-time," Al had replied, "whether in the sense of Inconsistent—like Thou shalt not shoplift except from large chain stores?—or in the sense of Provisional and/or Temporary, like Who were we kidding that it's okay to steal within limits? Anyhow, you won't be teaching TGB"—their shorthand for Lit & Phil's Truth, Goodness, and Beauty—"you'll be fixing their diction, grammar, spelling, and punctuation, and improving your own in the process. Relax and enjoy it."

He did, rather, once he'd met the two or three tutees with whom for the next six weeks he worked at one of several tables set up in what was meant to have been the rowhouse's living room. While other PTP's did similar repair work in other subjects at neighboring tables, and Levy himself held forth in his open-doored office to a select few on antidisestablishmentarianism and other sesquipedalia, Will pointed out misplaced modifiers, dangling participles, subject-verb disagreements, superfluous or missing commas, objective-cased predicate nominatives, and other such lapses in his students' high school English compositions, learning as he went along the names of those errors and the principles by them embodied, and improving by the way his own copy-editing skills. "In this next paragraph," he would explain to Ann Stein, daughter of a prominent local department-store owner, "when you say 'The Indians only hunted and fought on foot until the Spanish brought horses to America,' you imply that they did nothing else on foot, like just walking, or maybe dancing around the campfire. What you mean to say is that the Indians hunted and fought *only on foot* until et cetera. Okay?" Whereupon that sultry black-haired beauty (at seventeen, only a year younger than her precociously part-time preceptor), who drove from her private school sixth-form English classes down to Levy's Prep in a new canary-yellow Ford convertible, would roll her lustrous eyes and make the correction—not without grumbling that only an idiot would misunderstand what she meant. Likewise when Stanley Fine—curly-headed, mischief-twinkling scion of the city's Fine Laundry and Dry Cleaning chain—wrote "Turning the corner, the Empire State Building came into view," and Will observed that skyscrapers don't normally turn corners: "So if everybody understands it, what's the problem?" Considering that not-unreasonable question for perhaps the first time, Will responded experimentally to the grinning pair that a mother's understanding her child's baby talk is no justification for letting the kid remain at that primitive level of communication. "Weak analogical reasoning," Al would object that evening (and Will would duly report to his preceptees next day), "since nobody *except* Mom understands the kid, whereas et cetera. What you should've said is that misplaced modifiers and such are like static on the radio: objectionable even if we can make out what number the band's playing. We shouldn't have to get the message *despite* its wording."

"Aiyiyi," groaned Stein to Fine. "They really *dig* this stuff! Can you believe it?"

And Will, unbothered, "You'd *better* believe it, friends. Sloppy language equals sloppy thinking. Honor thy mother tongue."

Cheerfully retorted Fine, "Never mind our mother tongue, man; let's finish our mothering homework and get our tushies out of here."

For that was, as Al had forewarned, what Levy's preceptors were chiefly paid for: not merely to correct errors in their charges' homework assignments with a bit of instruction in the process, but to do those assignments for them, more or less, under the guise of tutelage. Hence the Freds' name for the place: the Cheatery.

"But it's more than just us helping the kids cheat their teachers and themselves," Winnie observed a week or so later, when Levy hired her after all to replace a PTP in French who'd quit without notice: "The kids are cheating their classmates by getting professional help that the others don't have. The parents who know what we're really up to are cheating both their own kids and the school system. And the ones who believe we're actually tutoring instead of cheating are being cheated by us."

"Also, contrariwise," Will pointed out, "the ones who're paying us mainly to cheat get cheated when some of us try mainly to teach."

What was more, they agreed, Lou Levy was cheating the parents by representing his preceptors as graduate students, and cheating both by charging five dollars an hour, paying the PTPs two, and pocketing the other three himself—a tidy profit, by the Freds' estimation, even after allowing for building upkeep and other overhead expenses—all the while maintaining that the institution was pedagogically proper and beneficial, indeed all but eleemosynary. It could even be argued, they enjoyed supposing, that in at least some instances the kids' official teachers were cheating all hands with make-work assignments designed primarily to satisfy the Procrustean requirements of curriculum planners and to compensate for indifferent classroom teaching.

"So what are we doing here?" Win asked Will, taking his hand in hers on the uptown bus ride home a few days into their joint preceptorships. "Who the fuck do we think we are?"

As to the first of those questions, it was Al Baumann's subsequently delivered opinion that in time-honored 3F fashion they were exploring moral ambiguities, experimenting with ethical parameters, honing their language and editorial skills, and scoring two dollars apiece per hour, all to the end of clarifying, if not necessarily answering, Question Two. "More to the point," Will in turn asked Winnie as that pair sat hip to hip on his Murphy-bed edge in Briarwood 204 after their two-hour gig at the Trivium at the close of that same April Friday evening, about to consummate his sexual initiation and (he supposed with guilty excitement) her first sexual infidelity, and she reported her "part-time fiancé's" reply, above, to their bus ride questions, "What are we doing *here?* Who do we think we are?"

Same answer, no doubt, his naked friend and colleague supposed. What *she'd* like to know (picking up his hand again, placing it firmly between her legs, and declaring "It's yours") is why it was always she who had to take the lead with him, as she'd done once again by knocking on his door a short while ago and brisking past him into his apartment, announcing cheerily as she peeled off her robe and pajamas that it was class time for Fornication 101. "You're supposed to *set* the beat, not follow it."

As to that, dazzled Will would remind her presently, in their combo it was Al, ever their leader, who set the beat from his stance between them at his bass—"A-*one*, a-*two*, a-*one-two-three-four*"—and himself who then maintained it, kept it up.

"So keep it up!" she urged, implored, commanded from beneath him, her eyes winced shut, head whipping from side to side as if in happy pain. "It's *yours*, Will! Go to it!"

He duly went and shortly came, his instrument unsheathed except by hers in their *duetto agitato* ("Leave precautions to me," she had instructed him while demonstrating Insertion of Diaphragm: "I'm the one who gets the bill if things go wrong"), and did likewise repeatedly through that spring, deliciously by her preceptored in intercourse digital, oral, vaginal, and anal, in a repertoire of positions and with assorted refinements, usually but not always on post-Trivium Friday nights in his apartment. "Jesus, Win," he groaned into her not-*quite*-equiangular Y at one point during that first of them, as she was tutoring him in *soixante-neuf:* "Al's the best friend I ever had! Best teacher! Best coach!"

To his scrotum she responded, "Mine too, dummy—and has been for ten times longer."

"So . . . ?"

Raising herself on one elbow, "D'you think he doesn't know I'm here, and what we're doing?"

"He does?"

Her sex-wet, fragrant thighs clamped shut. "Did you think I was *cheating* on him? Wait'll I tell him!" He had all but *ordered* her there, she declared—not that she objected to her assignment: the capital-P Protagonist's capital-I Initiation into the ditto-M Mysteries.

Lucky protagonist, to have so able an initiator. No beauty, Winifred Stark, with her too-plump cheeks and less-than-slender waist and legs; but she was high-spirited, amused and amusing in and out of bed, while also impassioned: an altogether admirable part-time preceptor. And Al clearly *did* know, at least in a general way, and evidently accepted, what his trio-mates were up to in their *ménage à deux et un peu,* as he himself came to call it on the infrequent occasions—over dinner or between sets at the Trivium—when the subject was lightly alluded to. Did he also know that as his protégé-protagonist's sexual self-confidence increased, Will would sometimes importune his initiator, en route home to Briarwood from the Cheatery, to detour into 204 for a quickie, perhaps even a not-so-quickie, before she continued upstairs? And that Winnie seemed pleased by these impromptu detours—"intromission times," she liked to call them—to the point of occasionally arching an expectant eyebrow himward as their elevator reached floor 2? That it was she who forbade him to sheathe his *grand peu,* as she saw fit to call it ("*plus grand* than some other *peux* in this *ménage*"), even when she was *sans* diaphragm, as was generally the case in these unscheduled come-togethers, bidding him instead to withdraw at the last pre-climactic moment and ejaculate instead into her navel or any other nonvaginal receptor? One imagined not, though with Al Baumann there was no telling.

Face-down in Will's pillow at a Wednesday afternoon's end, her pink butt elevated for their mutual pleasure, "Who knows what our Amazing Al knows and doesn't know?" Win would ask rhetorically. "The guy knows such a shitload!"

"He *didn't* know, Reader," those couplers' mentoring spirit here interjects. "At least not in any face-down-in-Will's-pillow detail, although he half suspected something of the sort, swallowed hard, and did his best to shrug his Burgundy-bottle shoulders thereat. While his part-time fiancée was presenting her plump pinkery to his protégé's *plus grand peu, her* PTF was ears-deep in the dissertation that he aimed to finish in time for their spring 1950 wedding: a thesis not on the Myth of the Birth of the Wandering Hero, but on the Birth of the Myth thereof. More precisely, on its *re*birth for twentieth-century Modernists like James Joyce, T. S. Eliot, *et alii* after Sir James Frazer's groundbreaking *Golden Bough* of 1890, and its culmination in such landmark studies as Lord Raglan's, Bronislaw Malinowski's, Joseph Campbell's, and, one had innocently hoped, Alfred Baumann Ph.D.'s, that erstwhile Friday-night wittol and subsequent impromptu cuckold. Pardon the footnote?"

Footnote pardoned, O best of mentors—whose culminative dissertation was fated never to see the publication it eminently deserved, nor its author his post-doctoral full-time academic appointment and ensuing, assuredly brilliant professorial career.

"Aborted, like some other things. But before we get to *that,* permit said nipped-in-the-bud dissertator to remark aside that thus far into this Three Freds Story its narrator has neglected to mention, among other things, any of Will Chase's other VVLU classes, seminars, and workshops besides Lit-Phil and Yarnspinning One-oh-one, or any other-than-Fred friends, classmates, and professors, some of whom surely must have *impacted,* as they say, his vocation? Nor has he, for the sake of verisimilitude and capital-T Texture, gotten into the nitty-gritty of our weekend music-making at the Trivium, as might have been expected. Too busy choosing ejaculatory receptacles?"

Too busy crying *Fuck Fate!,* which so roundly fucked good Al Baumann.

"Leave *that* ejaculation to Fate's fuckee, friend, and get on with Will and Winnie's getting it on. *Tell Me.*"

Ro-*ger,* Teach: Brit slang, Narrator believes, for what

that pair were energetically up to, more or less behind their best pal's back. Will rogered Win, Win Will, all over B 204, and B 304 as well when her One True Love was off in the library stacks comparative-mythologizing, as he often was. Even rogered her *there* one mid-summer Monday eve, he did, or she him, up against a carrel in the farthest alcoves of Sanskrit Lit—decoupling in the nick of time, or nearly, to spritz the gilt-lettered spines of the *Panchatantra* instead of Ms. Stark's unshielded privity.

"The Ryder translation, that would have been, one wagers: 1925."

If you say so, boss. Yet let it not be supposed that these goers-to-it *loved* each other, or that their busy erotic/moral experimentation was shame-free. *Bonded* they were, for sure—mainly by their joint esteem for Win's One True Et Cet—but what they felt for each other was friend-love, nowise lover-love. And while their shared appall at their infidelity was no doubt an added spice to those non-Friday clandestineries, it was nonetheless stingingly authentic shame, of the what-the-fuck-are-we-*doing?* variety. "Sexual errancy in general," Al Baumann liked to tell his Lit & Phillers when their syllabus reached Tolstoy and Flaubert, "and adultery in particular, are to the nineteenth-century social-realistic novel what Fate and hubris are to Greek tragedy: the mainspring of the action. Oedipus innocently but not unintentionally nails his dad at the Place Where Three Roads Meet, fulfilling the very prophecy that he was in flight from; Anna Karenina and Emma Bovary drop their extramarital drawers. In both genres, it's on with the story."

Which is to say, in the errant Freds' case, on to the next turn of the plot-screw, excuse the expression.

"Expression excused, friend. Likewise plot-screw, while I'm at it: unforgotten, mind, but truly long since forgiven, as it would be even if I hadn't brought it on myself with that Friday-night Share the Goodies routine—*my* bright idea, though Win didn't need much persuading. And it's time those horny young cheats forgave themselves. Maybe that's what's going on here?"

Not for Teller to presume.

"Anyhow, man, on with it: Eternity doesn't last forever; it only seems to. Turn that screw!"

Pause. Sigh. Screw that turn, Al: Can't do it.

"You fucking *must;* otherwise it'll be *my* turn to tell and our story's turn to get screwed. *How through that spring and summer of 'forty-nine, the season of the Cheatery—while the new state of Israel celebrated its first anniversary, and Mao Tse-tung's Red Army drove Chiang Kai-shek's Nationalists out of China, and the USSR maintained its Berlin blockade while preparing to test its first A-bomb, and North Korea made ready to invade South—all three Freds went at it like the variously gifted, high-energy young screw-ups they were,* dot dot dot et cetera. *Tell* me."

. . . by no means *merely* rogering one another literally and figuratively, busy as they were at that. Much more busily, in fact, they were (in Winnie's case) pursuing mastery of both the pianoforte and the Science of Libraries; in Al's, taking unto himself the *rest* of the corpus of Comparative Mythology and related disciplines while also teaching Adult Ed classes in the university's night school, prodding Will through the long list of texts he'd better have under his belt if he aspired ever to add something of his own thereto, and also coaching him in the Proper Percussionist's paradiddles, flamadiddles, flamacues, and other such licks that Will used routinely in their Trivium sessions without knowing the terminology—

"*The way Molière's Monsieur Jourdain,* you're expected

to say at this point, *discovers he's been speaking Prose all his life without knowing it.* Tell on."

And in said percussor's case, practicing likewise with Bassist Baumann's assistance the cues and diddles of narrative sentence-making, plot construction, character and scene rendition—

"Insofar as one without those knacks can aid one with."

Which is to say, considerably. And over and above all this cue-and-diddling, or in its interstices, Ann Stein and Stan Fine (and Jim Murphy, Jean Wallace, and half a dozen other Lou Levyites) not only got their homework assignments virtually done for them by their two-buck-an-hour virtual grad-student part-time preceptors, but were by them genuinely preceptored as well: some rather much, some only slightly, depending on their own receptiveness, but none not at all. Enough anyhow so that toward summer's end Headmaster Levy declared himself prepared to make it worth Will's and Winnie's while to stay on, "with a not-inconsiderable pay raise," come fall.

"But the fall came early that year, as I remember. July, was it? August?"

3. *"TELL ME"*

One early-June-'49 Friday evening in Briarwood 304, as she and Alfred Baumann were introducing Wilfred Chase to beef fondue, with which, like many another civilized item, he was unfamiliar, "Did you-all know," Winifred Stark asked her male colleagues/companions/lovers, "that the triangle—by which I mean the humble chrome-steel musical instrument, not the rusty old mainspring of Romantic fiction—despite its being the smallest and simplest bit of hardware in the orchestra, can make its ding-a-ling heard through the sound of all the other symphonic instruments combined? Just thought I'd mention that."

"Mm-hm," said their Near-Boy (the VVLU graduate-students' term for doctoral candidates otherwise classified as ABDs, they having completed All [of their degree requirements] But [their] Dissertation[s]) Baumann. "And apropos of what, exactly, does our winsome Win-Win offer her Fred-friends this musicological tidbit?" Which had been prompted by their Friday-evening pre-dinner custom, in lieu of either Christian table-grace or Jewish Sabbath-prayer, of rubbing wet index-fingertips in concert around the rims of their half-filled wineglasses to make them sing in ethereal near-unison before clinking same and commencing the meal.

"You tell *me,*" the ruddy lass invited, then demonstrated to webfoot Will how one speared a cube of raw beefsteak with one's fondue fork and plunged it into the Sterno-fired cooking-oil pot before dipping it into one of the several *garnis* ranged palette-like around one's plate.

"To me," obliged her fascinated preceptee, "that penetrative ping sounds like a simile waiting for its other shoe to drop—pardon the mixed figure."

"Not *mixed,* actually, in this instance," corrected ABD Al. "*Compounded,* maybe?"

"Like a felony?" Win wondered, at the same time teaching Will by example that one's place setting was provided with two long-shafted fondue forks so that one's next beef bit could cook while its now-done predecessor was garnished and eaten.

"Simile upon simile!" that greenhorn marveled. "We're three-deep now, by my count; want to go for four?"

"In your resident Near-Boy's considered opinion," put in Al, "mixed-metaphoric triangles should be compounded no more than thrice. Let's quit while we're ahead."

There was upon this banter a palpable voltage—as if, so it felt to Will, his fondue-mates were on to something that he was not, of a character more mattersome than the timbre of chrome-steel triangles, the compounding of tropes, or the oil-boiling of beef. As if, moreover, each of those two knew something further that the other did not, at least for certain, yet. Unsophisticated as he was in many a department, young Narrator-Aspirant Wilfred Chase had some feel for interpersonal voltages.

"As to *that,*" next declared Winnie—"I mean quitting while we're ahead?—I suspect it's too late already." Dinging then her fondue fork on the pot rim as if signaling the room's attention, "Bombshell time, everybody!" she announced, and went on to report that for the very first time since her menarche at age fourteen, she had, just a fortnight past, missed one of her regular-as-moonphase menstrual periods. Should she similarly, a fortnight hence, skip her next, one or the other of her fellow fonduers was an expectant father, the odds being by her estimate between three and five to one in the Three Freds' bassist's favor, "and what in God's *name* are our parents going to say when we tell them?" Teary-eyed now, "And what the damn *hell* are we going to do?"

When stunned Wilfred had regained his breath, if scarcely his composure, he inhaled deeply, closed and then opened his eyes, dinged one of *his* brace of fondue forks in like manner, declared "My turn now," and to Al (who'd seemed not at all startled by Winnie's announcement) confessed that, other things equal, the paternity odds were in fact shamefully closer to fifty-fifty than to five or even three to one, himself and Winnie having been at it over the past two months rather more often than on their Al-allotted, post-Trivium Friday nights. He, for one (but he was sure Win felt the same), was contrite at their having so abused the generosity and trust of the best, most valued friend he'd ever had. "I feel like absolute shit, man."

Too angry now for tears, "You *are* absolute shit!" affirmed Winnie. "Squealing on us without giving me a chance to come clean first!" For a moment she seemed ready to attack Will with her fondue fork; then she flung it down instead and buried her face in her paper dinner napkin. "You *shit!*"

"Ding-ding, guys," wearily here interjected Al, and rapped *his* fork now on the fondue pot like (Will could not help noting to himself) the aforefigured triangle sounding through the rest of the orchestra. "My turn in the bombardier's seat now?"

Before adding his tuppence to this dinner-table truth-telling session, he then calmly declared, he wanted to remind his tablemates once again that this Friday-night *deux et un peu* Al/Win/Will routine had been *his* questionable idea in the first place, in his self-assumed role of Hero's Helper; if it had gotten out of hand, as he'd lately been pretty much aware that it had, he supposed he deserved the consequences. In a parody of his classroom lectorial voice, he reminded all hands further that his use of the term *hero* in this context by no means implied a conviction on his part that young Willie Chase of Blue Crab County was destined to do Big Things. Among its other parallels, the Wandering Hero shtick was just Everyman's story writ large, or nearly every man's; the odds against any given Young Talent's grandly fulfilling its promise were in his opinion comparable to those against any given spermatozoon's thrashing successfully upstream through its swarming fellows and nailing the ovum, pardon his analogy. What he'd come to feel, and strongly—a preoccupational hazard, he supposed, given his dissertation topic—was merely that Comrade Chase, despite whatever shortcomings in the sophistication way, belonged distinctly in the category of Swimmer, and himself, just as distinctly, in that of Coach-Facilitator.

Shrieked Winnie, "Would you stop it already with the sperm and eggs? I'm *pregnant,* damn it! Knocked up!"

"Quite possibly." Taking her hand across the table corner, "And when we know for sure, we'll deal with it."

Steadier now despite her tears, What did he mean *deal with it*? she wanted to know—as, very much indeed, did Will.

Their companion shrugged. "Either we move up our wedding date and make the kid more or less legit, or we consult Matson," Winnie's gynecologist, a colleague of Al's father, "about fixing it for us, if that's what we'd prefer. And if Matson declines," these being pre–*Roe v. Wade* days, when abortion was still officially prohibited in the US of A, "we fess up and ask Dad for suggestions."

"What's this *if* we'd prefer?" But she didn't snatch back her hand. "D'you think I want a kid that might even *possibly* not be yours? I'm not ready even if it *is* yours!"

Patting her his-held hand with his other, "So we have ourselves a chat with Doc Matson when the time comes. *But*—as I was saying?" He dinged the pot again for attention and resumed his mock-lectorial tone: "What we-all find ourselves presently approaching on the not-so-merry-go-round of the Heroic Cycle"—he indicated by fork each Fred in turn: "Hero-Aspirant *malgré lui* or anyhow Protagonist *in potentia,* Prematurely Pronged Princess, and Has-Been

Helper—is the So Long, Sidekick scene, celebrated in song and story."

The first- and second-named of that triad froze in baffled apprehension, borderline alarm. *Has-Been? So Long?*

"Said Sidekick's *addio* aria," Al went on, "commences with his gently informing Miz Princess that the fruit of her womb, whether nipped in bud or nurtured to harvest, is almost certainly not of his planting, he having learned among other interesting things in a recent clinical workup (a) that his sperm count is low almost to the point of nonexistence, and (b) that roughly ninety percent of his paltry output are nonmotile. Ergo, guys, whether or not it's bye-bye baby this time next month—and I, for one, rather hope it won't be—the odds against its being Baumann's wee bastard in there are . . . what? About a quarter-million to one? Half a million?"

Too stricken to reply, Winnie pushed aside her plate and plopped her head face-down on the table before the bubbling pot. Soul-shaken Wilfred, suddenly more apprehensive than before, wondered, "So what *else* did the docs have to say, Al?"

Their bass-figured leader smiled at his questioner and then at Winnie (sitting upright again, face drained). Speaking as if to their clasped hands, "In a properly constructed story," he declared, "there'd've been a few strategically placed foreshadowings before now: I might've mentioned joint pains ten pages ago, for example, or you two could've remarked between fucks that old Near-Boy was looking weaker and paler in Part Two of this yarn than he looked in Part One . . ."

"Al?"

"At least we should've planted a little bleeding from

mouth, nose, and asshole—or, as the *Merck Manual* elegantly puts it, quote *thrombocytopenia giving rise to petechiae and ecchymoses* unquote." To Will, "Don't you love that lingo, man? You could have the guy's girlfriend find him reading the seventh-edition *Merck* one night in bed when she comes up from downstairs, and sort of wondering, What the fuck? But she figures it's just another of his gotta-know-everything things, so she nods off worrying about her period instead . . ."

"*Al!*"

Returning his fork to its intended use, their ariast (more pallid indeed, they noted now, than his never-ruddy usual) speared and dunked a final beef bit into the pot, just barely bubbling above its waning blue Sterno flame.

"Not A-L Al anymore, friends. From here on out it's A-*M*-L Al: Acute Myeloblastic Leukemia." And "here on out," he explained to his listeners too shocked to speak, meant possibly the whole upcoming academic year, if the methotrexate with which he was currently being dosed effected the brief remission that he much hoped for in order to wind up his goddamned myth dissertation, see his Part-Time Fiancée's Interesting Condition resolved one way or the other, and maybe goose his Ritual Wandering Whatchacallit-pal one step farther around the famous Cycle. "Otherwise, guys," which VVLU's oncological gurus, Dad Baumann included, had regretfully informed him meant Usually, "we're talking maybe four to six months. Sorry about that. But ain't Truth swell? I feel freer already."

Winifred Stark's entire hysteria; Wilfred Chase's groaning speechlessness; Alfred Baumann's calm consumption of the last of his beef cubes, washed down with the red jug-wine to which the Three Freds treated themselves on Friday evenings before repairing to the Trivium and thence et cetera: In time, perhaps, one would be up to rendering such things into language.

"One better fucking *had* be," now growls Al's ghost. "That's what you're fucking *for!*"

Well . . .

"Well, hell! Take it from the edge, as we musician types used to say: Tell the Three Freds Story over and over, damn it, till you get it right! Even *after* you get it right, if you ever do."

Yes, well, Al . . .

"Check our job descriptions, man: I did *my* thing, and then got my fat ass offstage on cue. Win did hers by spreading her legs for me and then for you and then for Doc Matson's D and C. So now you do yours: *Tell* me! Tell *us!*"

Narrator had aspired to do no less: the protracted though mercifully pain-dulled dying, which would have been expedited by suicide, friend-assisted or otherwise, but for Al's determination to press on to the end with the final-drafting of his Rebirth of the Ur-Myth thesis. Winnie's late-July dilation and curettage, assented to reluctantly by her fiancé but right readily by his contrite cuckolder, and performed discreetly by gynecologist Matson under the pretext, routine in those days, of removing a suspicious cervical lesion. ("That's taking the Imperiled Infancy thing a bit far, no?" Al joked wearily—all but bedridden then and about to be shifted, of necessity, from Briarwood 304 back to his boyhood bedroom in his parents' house, his hoped-for remission having proved only partial and his need of nursing care ever more pressing.) His quiet December expiration, with his dissertation's closing chapter—"Will He Return?"—still in revision. The Three Freds' subsequently going, like the arms of an equiangular Y, their separate ways: Al to the Baumann family grave plot in Lancaster, Pennsylvania; Winnie to a season of prostrate guilty grief and halfhearted psychotherapy, but then on to her college graduation after all, followed by a restorative summer in France with two Goucher classmates and a new life thereafter on North America's other coast, having nothing to do either with music (so Will heard through the Briarwood grapevine) or with her erstwhile fellow Cheatery preceptor—himself by then involved with another lover. Their Trivium-trio was replaced by a nameless electric-guitar/-bass/-keyboard outfit playing an overamplified new pop music called rock-and-roll, which its devotees predicted (absurdly, in Fred Three's mistaken opinion) would be to the century's second half what jazz in its several forms—Dixieland, swing, progressive, bebop—had been to its first.

And the nowise heroical Wilfred Chase? Still not yet twenty at the time here told of, just entering his junior undergraduate year at VVLU, he'll find that quite as he'd been shocked speechless by his Sidekick's Friday-night-fondue announcement of fatal malignancy, that irreplaceable comrade's dying will shock him, as it were, into speech—anyhow into a redoubled conviction of his calling, whether or not he proved capable of adequate response: an impassioned resolve to *tell,* not only Al Baumann's story, the Three Freds Story (trifles in themselves, and yet, and yet . . .), but also, though he could not then have put it into these words, the *story* of those stories. Maybe even somehow (rest in peace, bass-shaped buddy, while your determined tutee does his damnedest to keep the beat!) the capital-S Story's story, whatever *that* might be.

"Chances are, of course, he won't manage it," comments

ONCE UPON A TIME, I've been told, we Stories kicked off with "Once upon a time," or some other such Square One formulation, and then took it from there: Leda lays egg, egg hatches Helen, Helen lays Paris, Greeks lay waste to Troy, et cetera. Or, closer to home, "My name is I've Been Told. I began two sentences ago with *Once upon a time,* and here I am: wide-eyed hatchling, old as the hills but clueless as to who and where I might be this time and what'll happen next."

Not quite so. If some of my plain-folks ancestors (and some not-so-plain ones who for one reason or another wore Plainness as a camouflage) began as if straightforwardly at their "beginnings," others equally venerable thought it best to start off in the middle of things: *in medias res,* as Coach Horace famously put it, not *ab ovo* with the egg abovementioned. Which fateful ovum, be it noted, wasn't really the Troy tale's Square One anyhow, since in order for Ms. Leda to lay the thing, Zeus-in-swan-drag had to lay Leda, and back we go, chicken<egg<chicken<egg ad all but infinitum, to whatever Big Bang began Troy's tale and all the others. No, recommends Doc Horace: *Stories* may begin at their "beginnings," but their *tellings* commence where their Teller sees fit, and since all hands know the tale already anyhow (for what kind of loser would invent a *brand-new* story, and so distract the house with What'll Happen Next that they miss Teller's cool new riffs on the classic tune?), better start off in the next-to-last year of the War or the Wandering, and then with your left hand remind 'em of the Tale Thus Far while your right keeps the plot-pot bubbling toward full boil. You follow me?

Fact is, an old pro like Yours Truly can have it both ways: Once upon a time, e.g., there was a story that began not only in the middle of things but well past that middle, just a hop/skip/hobble from Climax and Curtain—and that story *c'est moi,* guys, and here's how I go, now that I've got myself cranked and more or less under way:

Who "I" am, see, is your world-renowned, ball-busting Myth of the Wandering Hero—but you can just call me Fred. Or Frank or Florence, Fiorello or Fiddle-Dee-Dee; I've used a thousand aka's, and none of 'em's me, so Fred'll do. Old-Fart Fred, let's say: the kind of Seedy Senior you might see straggling west along the shoulder of the interstate, long raggedy hair and beard, patchwork clothes like some displaced Robinson Crusoe's, all his earthly possessions in cruddy sacks slung over his shoulders, heedless of the SUVs and eighteen-wheelers roaring by, which aren't allowed to stop and offer him a lift even should they so incline. Which you can bet your bottom buck they don't, any more than *you* would—who, however, have been enough taken by the queer apparition at least to slow down, shake head, and wonder where in the wide world I'm coming from, and where headed and why, and how I got this way, and what I think of myself and the story of my life, and how I'll manage to scrounge my next meal out here on the eight-laner, and where I'll lay my flea-bit carcass down to sleep tonight. Thanks for that, Reader dear.

"Story of my life," did I just hear me say? And (somewhere back there) "I've been told . . ."? Boyoboy, friends, have I ever, a hundred hundred times over! Being told, you might say, *is* the story of my life and the life of my story; told over and over, whether by different tellers or by the same teller at different times and in different ways: straight up and slantwise, minimally and maximally, realistically and fantastically, comically and tragically—and as narrative or drama, in prose/verse/song, set in sundry locales at sundry "times" with sundry casts of characters, but under all those trappings the same old me, Same Old Story, starring same old Oedipus/Perseus/Odysseus/Aeneas aka Peripatetic Pete or Freaked-Out Fred, all of whom and a shitload more I've "been" and none of whom's *me,* as I may've mentioned already, inasmuch as I'm no really real person (granted, we all feel that way now and then) nor even "really" a Fictional Character like those hero types abovementioned. Fact is, friends, I'm a fucking *fiction,* know what I'm saying? Just an old-fart *story,* maybe the oldest in the books—but let's just call me Fred. If I seem to ramble here and there, that may be because I ramble here and there, as geezers will. Or it may be (Reader take note) that I only *seem* to ramble, while actually getting a bunch of that left-hand business done.

O.-F. Fred, then, whose Whole Story compriseth no

fewer than four full "acts," although various of my tellers have contented themselves with just one or another thereof. If you know the drill already, skip this paragraph. If not, let me remind you that I "begin" (you know what I mean) with my star-of-the-moment's Unusual Conception (Mom a Royal Virgin, literal or figurative; Dad rumored to be a God, ditto) and Imperiled Infancy (Threat and Rescue, Wound and Scar—the last of those useful for later ID); his Obscure Childhood "in another country" (lit. or fig.); his eventual Summons to Adventure; his Setting Out with help of Helper (and/or magical Weapon, Token, Password), bound either Homeward or Bottom-of-Thingsward or both, and his loss of Way/Weapon/Sidekick/Whatever as he approaches or crosses the Threshold of Adventure, from Daylit Waking World to Twilight Zone. Sound familiar? I should hope so, unless you were born yesterday (in which case, watch your back, kid, and keep your guard up). My Act Two? Obstacles and Adversaries! Riddles and Combats! Tests and Trials of every sort and size, overcome with help of re-found Helper or whatever else my guy lost back there at the Threshold. Descent to Underworld's dark heart; slaying of ultimate Dragon or Ogre; penetration of Mystery's innermost sanctum and/or of Captive Princess's. Sacred Marriage, is what I'm saying: mystical Illumination, consummate Consummation, Transcension of Categories, unmediated Knowledge, and like that? No wonder (Act Three) the bloke often needs goosing out of bed and back on course: a Summons to Return home-baseward from the Axis Mundi, delivered just about one-eighty around the Heroic track from where he got his original marching orders. So back upstairs he goes, maybe with Ms. Pronged Princess in tow or some other souvenir from the Bottom of Things, and maybe shifting shapes and costumes en route to give pursuers the slip, so that when (Act Four) he recrosses through Customs to the World Upstairs, he may be either in drag or else so morphed by his Adventures Thus Far that the homeland-security folks draw a blank till he flashes his afore-established Scar or other unequivocal ID. Which done, he Routs the Pretenders, assumes his rightful place as his hometown's Chief-in-Chief (or founds a New Burg, either on a hilltop or, like a stop-at-nothing real estate developer, in a marshfill), lays down the Law, and rules the waves, so to speak—he having, so to speak, waived all the rules—for, oh, eight years or thereabouts? Couple of Olympiads, let's say, or U.S. presidential terms? Anyhow, until he wakes up one not-so-fine morning to find himself and his administration inexplicably Fallen from Favor with gods and parishioners alike: the old magic flown, his authority kaput. Nothing for it, *tant pis,* but Exile (voluntary or otherwise) from his City, and the lonely trudge toward his Mysterious Finis—most often in a Sacred Grove, so I'm told, on a more or less Magic Mountain or at least a Spooky Hilltop, not unreminiscent of the Square One site of his Unusual Conception. Where his remains remain, nobody's certain, but several towns claim that touristical attraction. Some say the chap's not *really* dead, just taking a sabbatical leave from Heroing. Some swear that he'll be back, one of these days.

Heard that tune somewhere before, have you, luv? Then it should come as no surprise that after so many remakes and reruns I find myself "identifying," as they say nowadays, with my Protagonists: those serial slam-bangers from every age and culture who after a while amalgamate into one, and whose story becomes *my* story. Consider, s.v.p.: Mom a Virgin Queen and Dad a Maybe-God? You'd better believe it; how else did I get to be the Boss-Man Story I am, or anyhow was? Oldest in the book, first out of Ma Muse's womb and lord of the litter, sired by we-might-as-well-say Divine Imagination. And as for Imperiled Infancy and the rest, what tale's *not* in mortal danger till its testicles descend and it finds its voice? Which is to say, its Sidekick/Helper—in my case, the ablest yarnspinners on Planet Earth, whose words have been my Magic Passport. Obstacles and Adversaries? Try book burnings and other censorships, lost manuscripts and sacked libraries, whole civilizations destroyed or petered out, not to mention trivialization, Disneyfication, bumbling bards, and other such hazards. I marvel that I'm here at all! But upon my own Princess/Queen, the Muse of Archetypes, I've sired a worldwide web of Guys-Like-That tales, codified and commentaried by mythologers and pedants of every stripe.

A not-bad career, in short, and over its long course each episode in turn has been the one that seemed most Me-like. Until recently that had been the Triumphal Reign bit, from which I would look back with proprietary satisfaction (and not a little headshaking relief) at those harrowing earlier installments—just as, in ages past, I'd looked *forward,* eagerly, to the episodes ahead, while feeling most akin to Endangered/Abandoned Tot, Fledgling Adventurer, Full-Fettled Dragonslayer/Princess-Penetrator, and Returnee-in-Disguise about to rout Pretenders and reclaim Throne. Each in turn, I say, has felt like Where I'm At; 'tis a symptom of encroaching old-fartity, I don't doubt, that a time came when I found it ever harder to see myself as Oedipus the Rex, Odysseus the Suitor-Slayer, Aeneas the Empire-Founder, the Ur-Tale Victorious. What I got to sensing instead was . . . oh, I don't know: something like a fidget in the audience? As if the old shtick were losing its shine, like one of those smash-hit TV sitcoms that's dulled its edge because it's become its own adversary: its own hardest act to follow, if you follow me. So *many* dead Dragons, routed Pretenders, punctured Princesses and newfounded Cities —who needed yet another? It wasn't the Perseuses and Aeneases I came to feel most akin to, but the Lears and Prosperos: "my magic all o'erthrown," my City urban-blighted and suburban-sprawled, my Laws crusted and clotted with niggling amendments and commentaries-on-commentaries. Budget deficits, creaking infrastructure, cabinet ministers and heirs at sixes and sevens, calls for impeachment, even, and the barbarians arming out in the boonies! So okay, you might say: Who *doesn't* sometimes feel like a stranger in his/her own house, her/his own skin? But with O.-F. Fred it was no longer "sometimes."

Truth to tell (and we myths *do* that, believe us or not, in our old-fashioned fashion), I got to feeling just about ready to hang it up, pack it in, bid the homefolks *hasta la vista,* and clear out of here; hobble offstage while I could still hobble, and hit the old road again, to wherever. There's that Hilltop I'd so often told or been told of, somewhere Out Yonder; maybe it was time for me to trudge thataway? But I couldn't help half wishing—just reflex, I suppose; long-established habit—that I could pull off one more Biggie before I bowed out; close my curtain with a bang. Problem was, even we big-boss mythic-wandering-hero-tale types can't dream up our own specifics and tell ourselves: We need a particularizer, a reorchestrator, an inventive sidekick/mouthpiece—in a word (dot dot dot) a *Teller.*

So, Reader/Listener/Fellow Traveler: You know now who I am and where I'm coming from, right? What in the storytelling business we call the Exposition. And you've learned where I'm at at the time I tell of and what my capital-P Problem is—my Ground Situation, if you will: "a more or less voltaged state of affairs pre-existing the tale's Present Action," as they say in Taletelling 101. So you needn't be in the biz yourself to guess what's supposed to happen next: the famous *And then one day* that shifts narrative gears from the general and habitual to the specific and different; the novel element, character, or turn of events that introduces what we old hands call the Dramatic Vehicle, whose job (pardon the tech talk) is to precipitate a Story out of that afore-established Ground Situation.

Ready? You couldn't be more so than was Call-Me-Fred, whose all-'round out-of-it-hood reaches the point (now it can be told) where he packs his Narrative Bags (a-moldering on the shelf for lo these many seasons) and bids family and disaffected citizenry bye-bye. Hits the figurative road, does Figurative Fred; slips incognito out of town, as it were, looking not unlike that Seedy Senior on the interstate afore-invoked. But he gets no farther than—oh, some Place Where Three Roads Meet, shall we figuratively say? Pauses there to scratch head/arse/whatever; sits himself down (on a handy rock-seat smack in the middle of that fabled intersection) to Consider—and here I sit yet, as if at a bus stop in mid-Nowhere, talking to myself whilst awaiting my Dramatic Vehicle. Back yonder, the once-impressive ramparts of my City, cruddy now from deferred maintenance. Somewhere off either thataway or this, that consummatory Hilltop where et cetera. And over thisaway or that? Don't ask me, folks; I'm a stranger here myself.

And then one day . . . nothing happened? Nah, that was yesterday. Too many yesterdays.

And then one day . . . a certain Who-Knows-Whom chugs up in as high-mileage a queer old brokedown buggy as ever clunked down the narrative road. Sees me sitting there a-twiddling my thumbs and asks me, Need a lift? Depends, says I, all the while giving him and his beat-up three-wheeler (yup) the once-over, as did he me: Where you bound for? I couldn't tell for sure, vis-à-vis that idling not-so-hotrod, whether it was some antique Real McCoy or a high-tech trike in rattletrap drag. No two ways about its idling driver, though: a graybeard geezer like Yours Truly, plaid flannel shirt and worn-but-clean blue jeans; one whose experience and know-how, if such he had, might or might not make up for slowed-down reflexes and loss of muscle.

Damned if *I* know, says he—maybe honestly, maybe not, as his expression included a twinkle among its seams and creases. You look like a fellow who's been around the block a time or two: I was hoping you could tell *me* which road leads where.

To which I heard myself reply, Check out our job descriptions, Stranger: Telling's not *my* department. Anyhow, if you and these wheels are what I take you-all for, and if I'm what it suits you to have me be, then we both know what lies ahead no matter which way we go.

By which I meant, of course, Complication of Conflict, Escalation of Stakes, and general up-ratcheting of Action toward Climax and Denouement. In a word, the usual.

"I swear," swears he, with sigh and headshake as if I'd said that last aloud instead of to myself (and speaking now 'twixt quote marks as if to keep that distinction clear): "Just *thinking* about all that hassle's enough to tempt a guy to say Screw it, you know?" Left hand still on the wheel, he scrabbles with his right through the junk on his buggy's floor.

"Once upon a time I had me a six-pack in this old wreck somewhere. If I can find that sucker, I say let's set our butts down right here, pop ourselves a cool one, and shoot the shit a bit, okay? Let the Dragons and Princesses come to *us* for a change."

Says I, "Count me in, amigo"—no more quite meaning it than he did, was my guess—and I hauled over to his rolled-down window and stuck out my hand. "Name's Fred, by the way."

"Yeah, right." But gave it a squeeze. "Like mine's Isidore."

"Isidore?"

Grin: "Izzy for short—or Isn't he? You get the idea. And hey—" Opens half-stuck creaky driver's door with left hand while right holds aloft (like old Perseus brandishing Medusa's head, as I recall the scene) four-sixths of a pack of . . . uh, some cloudydark brew in unlabeled bottles with unmarked caps? Two of which—once he'd climbed out of his queer clunker and set himself and his trophy down on my bench-rock—he offed with the appropriate thingie on his Swiss Army knife. Then hands one bottle to me, a good fourth of it already foaming over from being either not chilled enough or not aged enough.

"Unlike you'n me, huh?" says he with stage wink behind his wire-rim specs, as if he could . . . well, read me like a book. "Some country boy's home brew, I reckon. Found it in that borrowed Vee-hickle. Here's to us?"

"Whoever *that* might be this time around. You leave your engine running?" For he'd made no move to turn it off.

Shrug. "More'n likely she'll run out of gas. Like us? But once you shut down an old fossil like that, who knows if it'll ever start up again." Raising his bottle, "You joining the party?" and takes a proper pull. As did I then, and resumed my place on the bench, the now two-pack between us.

Not a bad brew, considering.

"Thought you might think so. And *on the bench* pretty much sums us up, right?"

Speak for yourself, *Isidore,* said I to myself, there being evidently no need to speak aloud: Me, I've got an inning or two yet to play before I leave the field.

"Sez you," says he, but amiably, and adds, "Sez me too, pal. And like as not we're a brace of bullshitters, but I for one am in no rush to find that out."

Says you, *pal,* says I, likewise amiably: If I'm not mistaken, that's mainly why you're here.

"Mistaken you're not," allows he, and takes another pull of that yeasty world-temp brew. "No more'n half, anyhow. I'm here to find out where we go from here, same as you, but be damned if I'm in any hurry."

"Same as me"—speaking in quotes now, I see, same as he—and did same as he, and there we sat: Old-Fart Tale and ditto Teller, the one retold so many times that he doubts he has an encore left in him, the other having told so many that he doubts the same, but both with a half-assed hankering for Just One More before the narrative bar shuts down for keeps.

"Speaking whereof," says Mr. Call-Me-Izzy, and fishes out his handy-dandy again to uncap "what we can't rightly call our Last Drafts, can we now, seeing's how *they're* not on tap and you'n I are still in First Draft. If you follow me?"

Well, I didn't at first, but then did, sort of; enough anyhow to pick up on that *follow me* business and say, "This time you got the job descriptions right, bro: I go where you tell me, so I'm told."

"Beg to disagree." But cordial clink of bottles, swig of contents, and wipe of mouth on back of hand before declaring, "Seems to me it's you go *and* I tell you: tell the folks Out There where you went, and went next after that, and what did en route."

Says I, "Whatever"—whereupon Pal Izzy intones, "*And there they sat, and maybe sit yet: two bumps on the narrative log*. Seems to me," still him talking, "that like it or not, we're what they call *made for each other*?"

I considered that proposition. Whatever it'd been before, the landscape round about our intersection was a flat plain now, as featureless as—

"A Samuel Beckett stage set?" offered my—

"Self-Appointed Sidekick?"

Yes, well. As I was remarking, there were only the two roads forking oblique left and oblique right, straight to the bare horizon, at equal angles to each other and to the road behind—which once upon a time had led to and from Home Base, but now (when I glanced back that way), to my surprise, stretched likewise to the three-hundred-sixty-degree Out Yonder.

"From all of which one infers," inferred Sir Self-Appointed, "that there's been some Narrative Movement, shall we say? You're farther down the capital-R Road than you were before I drove up, and methinks that's *because* I drove up, in yonder bucket-o'-bolts Dramatic Vehicle."

"Do tell."

With conspiratorial elbow-nudge, "My job description, right? Who not only, in driving up, assumed *ipso facto* the role of Sidekick Helper, but in due discharge of that classic role supplied nonplused Hero with better-than-nothing Magic Potion plus handy-dandy Tool/Weapon/Whatever"—

indicating in turn the now-empty brew bottles and the now-pocketed Swiss Army gizmo wherewith he'd earlier flipped their lids—"and ready-for-action tricyclical DeeVee. In return for which, thankee, you've got me Telling now a mile a minute, who just a few pages back was wondering whether I had anything left to tell!"

"And not only telling," I started to say, "but—"

"Taking words *out* of your mouth instead of putting 'em in? I know, I know: Forgive me that, man"—smacks me upside the near shoulder—"it just feels so damn *right* to be back in action again, you know?"

So I'm told, said I, unless he said it for me: Putting pedal to the metal on one of those DV contraptions can do that to a fellow. Been there myself.

"And time to go again!" cries he—*exclaims, exuberates,* whatever, up off our bench and on his feet. "Before old Lizzie runs dry."

Like us?

"Speak for yourself, friend—so to speak? And never mind job descriptions from here on out: We're in this together."

Mm-hm. In *what,* exactly?

Tugs my coatsleeve. "*In medias res,* man, soon's we climb aboard. You drive the Herocycle; I'll narrate the blow-by-blow."

Um . . . ?

"Okay, okay: You drive; I'll narrate *and* navigate as needed. Nudge things along. *Sidekick* 'em, let's say."

Like for instance (we're in his not-all-that-Dramatic Vehicle now, his quote Herocycle, and I tell you this in parentheses because my dialogue quotes seem to've gotten left back on that rock-bench with our empties), which way do we go, S.K.? Can't flip a coin, unless you happen to have a three-sided nickel in there with your Handy-Dandy.

He cranes his stringy neck to consider, or at least to seem as if considering, our options in turn. Adjusts his specs. Then says, "Well, now: Seeing's how *you* came here from Back There," indicating the road that once upon a time led from my City, a bit east of north from our conjunction, "and *I* came out of Left Field yonder"—left from that city's point of view, and a bit east of south from said conjunction—"I reckon we should head out yonder on The Road Not Taken—at least not by us, at least not this time out. Off we go?"

My turn then to consider, as H.C. Lizzie idled erratically and I checked out her four-on-the-floor transmission, her mostly nonfunctioning dials and gauges, stiff steering, too-soft brakes, and what-all. Back There was everyone I'd ever been, for better or worse: not Oedipus/Odysseus/Perseus/Aeneas & Co., but their *stories* (including old Don Quixote's, whose nag Rocinante was the four-legged equivalent of our sputtering, spavined three-wheeled Liz). Off yonder where she and her geriatric driver had rattled in from, if we take him at his word (and what else is he, Mr. S.K. Izzy, if not his words?), was every tale he'd told to date—no doubt including a few variations of Yours Truly in one getup or another, if he was like most of his ilk. Why rerun old footage from any of those once-upon times? What's more (you can do this on your watch dial, Reader, if you don't happen to have a compass on your Swiss Army knife), inasmuch as Where I'm Coming From lay more or less north-northeastward—five minutes past the hour, say, at the *1* on your analogue watch?—and where *he* came from lay south-southeastward at the *5* (or twenty-five past), Road #3 stretched out due west, straight into the sun just now approaching set at a quarter till: fit hour for our game's last quarter, and mine. No capital-H Hilltop in sight over there beyond the *9* on your watch dial, but "Maybe that's what makes the thing Mysterious," offered we-know-who: "Shall we go have a look?"

By way of reply I shifted Liz into first, eased out her cranky clutch, stick-shifted into second, and—so I'm being told!—*floored* that mother.

2

How come this part's labeled "2," some sharp-eyed nitpicker's bound to ask, when what went before it wasn't labeled "1"?

Time was, I could answer back, when "Fred" and I minded such p's and q's, but we're past that nowadays. Fact is, however (I might point out in my capacity as the guy's *faute de mieux* Teller this time around), that inasmuch as he, for one, couldn't've known there'd *be* a Part Two till he hit Lizzie's pedal and landed us on this side of yonder space-break, he couldn't've bloody known that where we were before was Part One of anything, could he now, mate? So just maybe it's Symbolically Appropriate, as they say, for Part One to stand unlabeled as such; and just maybe some of us with a card or two still up-sleeve knew that all along.

Further questions?

Needn't've asked, I guess: There's always one eager beaver with hand in air. How's that? You're wondering why the "I" in "1" was Call-Me-Fred, the Old-Fart I've-Been-Told Story, but here in "2" it appears to be Call-Me-Izzy, the Sidekick Teller?

Well, since you've asked: You may recall F. and me

a-hassling each other a bit about "job descriptions" back there in "1"? What the issue came down to was, does he do what I say, or do I merely say what he does? 'Twas a tricky enough matter back when "he" was Odysseus and "I" was one of Homer's bards: The sly guy finally gets home not because it occurred to me to make it happen, but because (as the whole house knew) that's how his story'd *always* gone, which "Homer" most memorably arranged so that hacks like "me" could invoke Ms. Muse to sing you the news (through us) with whatever riffs and flourishes we saw fit. Got that? Later on, when "he" becomes Aeneas, say, and "I" become Virgil, the game changes: Within the stretchable bounds of Roman folk tradition, A. does what he does because V. was inspired not only to dream up his doing it, but to write those imaginings down for all time in good Latin hexameters that are in large measure A.'s marching orders as well as V.'s artful report thereof: "*I* sing of arms and the man," goes Maestro Virgil's written score, not "Sing, O Muse," et cet. Come then to a "he" who's e.g. Don Quixote and an "I" who's Don Miguel de Cervantes Saavedra, everything "he" does he does because "I" say so: Although I pretend I'm just reporting the news from La Mancha, D.Q. shoots exactly the shots I call, exactly as I've seen fit to invent those shots and call 'em. Things don't get truly dizzy-making again until you get an "I" who's Mr. Mark Twain, say, and a "he" who's young Huck Finn *telling his own story first-person*—i.e., as an *I!* "You don't know about me without you have read a book by the name of *The Adventures of Tom Sawyer,*" etc. Yet even that comes down to a fairly simple division of labor, finally, between Author/Teller and Narrator, doth it not? Twain "records" Huck's report of what-Huck-did-because-Twain-imagined-and-put-into-

Huck's-words-Huck's-doing-so, right? Or, to put it another way, Author tells Reader Narrator's telling-to-Reader of Tale-made-up-by-Author.

A tad vertiginous, sure, but no problem! Nor any question who's finally in charge. But now—fasten seat belts, folks—suppose First-Person Narrator of story to be not only its principal character, but *It:* the Story itself, telling us itself itself! Who's in the driver's seat now, I ask you, leapfrogging space-breaks and barreling us westward lickety-split through a landscape thus far featureless perhaps for want of Narrator's supplying us with its features? Moreover, since Setting is an ingredient of Story, as are accessory characters like Yours-Truly-as-Sidekick and Dramatic Vehicles like three-wheel Lizzie, how can "I"-the-Narrator of "Me"-the-Story differentiate himself from them/us in order to tell you us (except, I suppose, as "I" might tell of "my" toes and fingers, "my" hopes and fears, "my"self . . .)?

Well: "I," for one, get dizzy just thinking about such things, and so while "Fred" was shifting our buggy's gears from first toward third, I took the opportunity to do the same with him, narrative-point-of-view-wise. It's still his been-told story being told, mind, and he's still It, but *I'm* telling you the sucker from here on out, at least this part of it/slash/him; otherwise we'd all go around in such who's-in-charge-here circles that the three of us would likely keel over from narrative vertigo, and old Story's story'd disappear up its own asshole: a Mysterious Consummation for sure, but not likely the one Fred has in mind.

Indeed, while I've got the mike, so to speak, with your permission I'll just fill in a few blanks and maybe redo a detail or two? To begin with (excuse the expression), Mr. Hero-cycle-Driver's name isn't "really" either Fred or I. B. Told, any more than mine is "really" Isidore/Izzy/S.K./Et Al., except insofar as all of us turn into the stories that we tell ourselves and others about who we are. Which, no doubt, we all do, more or less. For while it may be true, as has been wisely said, that "the story of your life is not your life; it's your story," it's also true that our stories have "lives": They grow or shrink in their recollection and retellings; they add or lose details, whole episodes and characters even, as they age—and that's before we get to their ever-shifting slants and interpretations, by "ourselves" and others. Some are stillborn, some short-lived; others are all but immortal (not to say interminable), enjoying or anyhow living serial lives, multiple simultaneous lives, lives resonant with avatars and reincarnations . . .

But never mind all that, for now: A story that'll serve as Fred's and mine here in Part Two of "A Story's Story" happens to be that of _____—which, the way *I* tell it, goes something like this:

_____'S STORY

Open any fair-size Anglo phonebook to the B's and you'll find a handful of entries last-named Blank. The word is, after all, just a from-the-French version of the more common English name White or German Weiss, with the added connotation, perhaps slightly negative, of that color's absence rather than its presence. In any case, one doubts that *Blank, Dr. Shirley M., D.D.S.* thinks of herself as any sort of absence, any more than *Weiss, Stanley B., C.P.A.* regards himself as particularly pale; most last names mean *something*, but most bearers thereof are indifferent to, if not ignorant of, such significance.

Name a Blank kid Phil, however, and he's in for trouble. Yet that's what Michael and Madeline Blank of State College, Pennsylvania, saw fit to dub their firstborn in the Eisenhowerian early 1950s: Philip Norman Blank, his first name Mike's late dad's, the second Maddy's *née.*

O comparatively innocent American time and place! Two cataclysmic world wars already history, the Korean War fought to armistice, and the Vietnam tarbaby only just beginning to attract U.S. fingers. The nation's traditional hard-liquor culture was in salutary mid-shift to wine, and although most folks still poisoned their lungs and others' with cigarette smoke even in college seminar rooms, such heavier-duty narcotics as heroin and cocaine—just beginning to be a problem in large-city ghettos—were all but unknown on American campuses and small-town streets, where even marijuana was uncommon. Redbaiting, witch-hunting, blacklisting, and loyalty-oathing there was aplenty, alas, in the same anticommunist political fever that piously inserted "under God" into the Pledge of Allegiance; the military-industrial complex flourished as Cold War supplanted hot, and the rest of the economy did all right too, though over everything hung the nightmare possibility that the U.S.-Soviet arms race could trigger nuclear apocalypse. But most Americans felt reasonably easy despite the new black-and-yellow Civil Defense signs on public buildings, the occasional neighbor's armed-and-provisioned bomb shelter, and vague though well-founded worries about radioactive fallout from atomic weapons testing.

No youngster, anyhow, was liable to lose sleep over such matters, especially at such remove as central Pennsylvania's Allegheny-nestled "Happy Valley," where the land-grant college after which the town was named (not yet a university in those days) turned out the commonwealth's next generation of engineers, foresters, agriculturalists, business administrators, "home economists," and schoolteachers in a farm- and forest-surrounded community whose chief employer was the ever-growing academic institution, and whose student population nearly matched its non-. A peaceful place, State College PA, except on football weekends: solid tax base, good public school system, and virtually full employment; no super-richies on the one hand and few dirt-poors on the other; enough input from faculty, students, and resident alumni to preserve it from acute small-town parochialism, and a freedom from urban problems that went far toward compensating for its geographical isolation and any lack of sophisticated big-city amenities. All in all, a good venue for raising children, and the Blanks—Maddy herself an elementary-school-teaching alumna of the college before and after her pregnancies, Mike a civil-engineering alumnus employed by the County Roads Commission—were more than content to raise theirs in its tranquil neighborhoods of laurel and rhododendron, its avenues of not-yet-blighted American elms.

Happy enough offspring of a happy enough couple, sturdy little Philip and baby sister Marsha, who came along two years later: like their parents, neither exceptional—physically, mentally, psychologically, or characterologically—nor deficient, except by comparison to the exceptional. No problems in the campus nursery school or the public school kindergarten; only in first grade did young Phil Blank's schoolmates, perhaps prompted by classroom exercises instructing all hands to *Fill in the blanks,* pick up teasingly on his name.

"They call me Phil-up the Blank!" he complained to his

parents one brilliant late-September Saturday, as the family's "pre-owned" Oldsmobile wagon climbed through hemlocked hills toward a state-forest lakeside picnic. "And sometimes just Phil the Blank, like I'm not there! Billy Marshall calls me Phil *N.* the Blank! I *hate* them!"

Dad's advice: "Forget it, pal. Teasing's part of every schoolkid's routine."

"Just remember how it feels," suggested Mom, "if *you're* ever tempted to tease somebody about their name or appearance or whatever."

"Your first and last names both are names to be proud of, son."

Mock-indignant Maddy then, "Not the middle?"

"Middle too!" her husband amended, and patted his wife's near knee. "For sure!"

"Did Grandpa get called Phil-up and stuff?"

Speaking to his son's image in the rearview mirror, "Not that he ever mentioned."

And Madeline, with a knowing small smile at her spouse, "Grandpa Phil was never one for mentioning things."

Their son then and there decided "I *hate* my name!"

"No!"

"I hate *my* name, too," offered four-year-old Marsha, who until that moment had never *thought* about her name.

"No you don't." Mom. "It's a lovely name."

"Is not." But in fact, like most people, she had no particular feelings about her name—her first name, anyhow—but simply accepted it as hers. As for *Blank,* while Marsha would be spared the degree of schoolmate teasing about it that her brother was subjected to, she wasn't sorry to abbreviate it to a middle initial nineteen Septembers later, upon her marriage.

Young Phil, however—although by second and third grade his classmates' jibes had become mere idle reflex—found himself unable to shrug off the twinge of dissatisfaction he felt at every roll call, every form that required him to fill its Name-blank with his Blank name. Neither popular with nor disliked by his fellows, he did his best not only to blend in but to . . . not *disappear,* quite, but to draw as little attention as possible to himself and thus to his awkward name, which by fifth grade he was determined to change as soon as he became "his own man": perhaps when he left home for college? Even before then, when pupils from the area's several neighborhood and township elementary schools came together in Centre County Junior High and High School, he experimented with *P. Norman Blank* and *Norman P. Blank*—"Norm for short," he informed his classmates, entreated his parents, and threatened his sister. But while his new teachers and classmates readily obliged, and his family did their best, most of his old classmates either forgot or declined to use his new name, and a few explained the old tease to their new comrades. The unhappy result was more rather than less attention to the tender subject; by the spring of his freshman high school year he was, for the most part, back to being called Phil Blank.

"Whoever *that* might be," he said to himself in effect, if not necessarily in those words; for as the CCHS class of '71's hormones kicked in and cranked up the ambient sexual voltage, and numerous of his schoolmates took their behavioral cues from the still-modest contingent of long-haired dope-smoking war-protesting hippie undergraduates over at the university (as the college became in the 1960s), Phil/Norm found it ever more difficult to decide who exactly he *was,* and to dress and behave accordingly. What he felt, but couldn't quite articulate even to himself, was that while one's name is not one's self (any more than one's life story is one's life), his peculiar name was a major determinant of his identity—whatever *that* might be. Its implicit directive—*Fill blank!*—led to both hyper-self-consciousness and abnormal self-uncertainty. The selves of his classmates seemed to him bone-deep and plain as day: Billy Marshall the taunting, newly hippie pothead and wannabe rock musician; Elsa Bauer the shy but not un-self-confident, really cute, and almost friendly sophomore class secretary, etc. His own self, on the contrary, seemed to him improvised, tentative, faint, and fluid: a masquerade. An act.

"Now, don't you worry," his mother worried when, in a moment of what had become unusual closeness between her son and anyone, he attempted to confide to her some of the above. "It's just a stage you're going through, honeybun. We all go through stages at your . . . you know . . ."

"My stage?"

And not long after, "Now, don't you worry, son," his dad embarrassed him by advising, which meant that Mom had blabbed the whole thing. "One of these days you're going to *be* somebody. That'll show 'em!"

"Yeah, right."

Kid sister Marsha—who in most respects seemed both to herself and to Philip to be the elder sibling—rolled her self-possessed eyes, but refrained from comment.

As if prompted by the conjunction of *an act, a stage,* and *be somebody,* in his latter high school years the young man found himself drawn to theater in general and the school's Drama Club in particular. Alas, although he tried out for a number of productions, it was apparent early on, to him and to the drama coach, that he had no notable thespian gift (compared, say, to Elsa Bauer, whose shyness miraculously vanished when she played another). He managed a few member-of-the-chorus roles—which, on reflection, he found more to his taste anyhow than being one of the play's principals. Even more he enjoyed sitting in the audience in a darkened hall and losing, in some film or stage play, the self that he'd never quite found.

He was, like the rest of his household, an indifferent secular agnostic who gave next to no thought to that noun or its modifiers. The Blanks celebrated Christmas, but observed no Sabbath, prayed no prayers, belonged to no church, and seldom spoke of religion. Son Philip, from age fourteen on, masturbated with about the same frequency as his male classmates, but had no way of knowing that. Managed a few dates in his junior and senior years—one with Elsa Bauer, who permitted him a ceremonial goodnight kiss but was already bespoken (by Billy Marshall) for the senior prom. Attended that function with Betsy Whitmore instead, a pleasant though plump and plain classmate of Marsha, who arranged the date. Neither partner much cared for dancing, but dance they duly did, a bit. Afterward, in the second seat of Billy's parents' two-tone green '69 Pontiac four-door, for appearances' sake they shared a reefer of marijuana and went through the motions of making out (he was permitted to squeeze his date's ample breast, under her blouse but not under her bra, and even briefly, with his other hand, to cup her crotch, under her skirt but not under her pantyhose—"And not a whit more," she seriously joked), to the distracting accompaniment of more vigorous grunts, moans, sighs, and thrashings in the vehicle's front seat. Betsy presently remembered a 1 A.M. parental curfew not previously mentioned; her date "called it an evening" too, forgoing the ritual sunrise breakfast at the class president's house after the all-night party at So-and-So's folks', out past the university's experimental farms.

"Talk about filling in the blanks!" Billy Marshall boasted next day re his and Elsa's front-seat shenanigans. Four years later, like several other high school classmate-sweethearts who elected to stay on at the local university instead of "going off" to college, that couple married, found suitable employment in the area, and raised their own brood in Happy Valley. Betsy Whitmore, however—with whom Phil more or less enjoyed one further date during the summer after his graduation—moved to Michigan with her family soon after, and the young pair did not maintain contact.

Philip himself, having done editorial and layout work on the staff of his high school newspaper, summer-jobbed as an intern with the county's *Centre Daily Times* and, without seriously considering alternatives, matriculated at "State" in September. His father had suggested a major in Business Administration as most likely to help a fellow without particular ambitions at least to earn a decent living, but did not protest his son's choice of General Arts and Sciences instead: "It's your life, not mine." His mother mildly approved: "Keeps your options open till you *find* yourself, you know?" Marsha rolled her eyes. Brother and sister were not at all close, but neither was there sibling rivalry or other ill will between them: Their relation was prevailingly cordial and passively affectionate, if somewhat stiff on Philip's part. She was not unhappy when after his freshman year he moved out of the house into the college dorms; but she defended, against her parents' complaints, his junior-year decision to change his name to Philip B. Norman. "Relax," she advised them. "At least he decided *something*."

For as a "Stater" herself and adjacent dorm resident by that time, she happened to know that her brother had experimented halfheartedly with changing not only his name and academic major (from General A & S to Pre-Law, then to Business Administration after all, and finally back to General), but his sexual orientation as well. "Hey, Norm," she telephoned him one football weekend after happening to catch sight of her brother and his College of Forestry roommate holding hands in a booth in the Corner Room Restaurant on College Avenue after the Syracuse game, "are you *gay* these days or what?" Unalarmed by her question, he guessed he maybe was: "Not a word to Mom and Dad, okay?" More surprised and amused than dismayed, "Not to worry!" Marsha assured him, and added, "Better gay than nothing."

But that "stage" lasted no longer than one academic term, whereafter "Phil Norman"'s briefly Significant Other found a roommate/lover more to his liking, and Philip himself became involved with a Poli Sci ex-lesbian as tentative about her sexuality as was he re his. In this same period —between spring break of his junior year and graduation time for the class of '75—ever-cheery Madeline Blank succumbed to metastasized uterine cancer, and her comparatively impassive but now-devastated husband to an evidently self-inflicted deer-rifle shot to the head not long after, in the same state park where the family had often picnicked in Philip's and Marsha's childhood. With a competence that he'd scarcely been aware of possessing, Phil made the arrangements for his dad's cremation and (per deceased's written request, in a terse note found on his body) the discreet dispersal of his ashes along the county roads to which he'd dedicated his working life.

Postponing his baccalaureate for one term, the young man then oversaw the settlement of Michael Blank's uncomplicated estate. Their father and mother having both been only children, Philip and Marsha were the sole surviving family members and equal heirs to their father's modest bank accounts, life insurance benefits, and property. The six-year-old station wagon went to Marsha, as Phil had his own car already; the proceeds from the family house (the sale of which Phil arranged through a local realtor who lived on their block), added to the rest of their inheritance, provided brother and sister with ample funds to rent small but comfortable and convenient apartments near the campus, to purchase whatever supplementary furnishings they needed after dividing their parents' belongings, and to support them comfortably through the remainder of their undergraduate studies and graduate school as well, if they elected to "go on."

Much shaken and saddened, though less than grief-stricken, by the loss of their parents, and feeling as much at home in the college town where they'd lived since birth as they'd felt in the house itself, they went on with their not-unhappy lives. Marsha's senior-year high school boyfriend, who'd done his first two college years in upstate New York, transferred to his hometown campus to complete his degree in Electrical Engineering as she completed hers in Education, and eventually moved in with his reignited old flame. Like Mike Blank and Maddy Norman (and Billy Marshall and Elsa Bauer), the couple married not long after their commencement and found employment in the area. Philip —who shortly after graduation re-changed his last name from Norman back to Blank and took a job in the university's public information office—reverted as well from an ambiguous bisexuality to less and less sexuality of any sort: To their mutual old acquaintances, "Nor-man nor woman," Billy Marshall joked, "equals Blank."

And blank his life might be said to have been, by many people's standards and sometimes his own, over the century's ensuing decades: a competent if undistinguished career in various of the university's administrative offices; one more sort-of-relationship, with a female office-neighbor several years his senior, whose rebound from an acrimonious divorce presently impelled her far from the region where her ex-husband chose to remain, and ended the affair—Phil's final experience of other-than-solitary sex, and on the whole an enjoyable one, for him at least. Occasionally he lunched with old acquaintances or administrative colleagues; most Sundays he dined with his sister and brother-in-law and their three children, whose uncle he was pleased to be despite his natural aloofness. Sometimes with them, more often alone, he attended varsity athletic events and university-sponsored concerts or theater productions. For exercise he walked the campus or the town's so-familiar neighborhoods; in the long Allegheny winters he sometimes worked out in the college gym. Most evenings he was content to dine alone in his apartment (later, his condominium in a new development north of town), read news-magazine articles for an hour or so, and then watch television or some video recommended by Marsha. If asked, he would not have characterized his life as unhappy, while acknowledging it to be far from full; but no one asked, and he himself, from his thirties on, gave ever less thought to such questions. His sister took vacation trips with her family, as did Billy and Elsa Marshall—to Florida, Maine, California, Hawaii, Europe. Philip's job sometimes took him to the university's branch campuses in sundry Pennsylvania counties and, less often, to meetings and conferences in Cleveland or Indianapolis, Ann Arbor or East Lansing; his vacations, however, he preferred to spend at home.

"Doing *what?*" Marsha's husband asked her once. His wife rolled her eyes, shook her head: "The Sunday *Times* crossword puzzle, maybe? Filling in the blanks, as Billy Marshall used to say."

In his late fifties, to Marsha's surprise and somewhat to his own, Philip elected to take early retirement. With his university pension, the dividends from sundry annuities, and his considerable savings, he would scarcely notice the reduction in his annual income. "Lucky fellow!" most of his child-raising, tuition-paying acquaintances agreed. "But what are you going to do with yourself?" his sister made bold to ask him.

A quarter-century earlier, Philip might have responded, "Do with whom?" But over the decades he had lost interest in that question. "Whatever I damn please, I suppose," was his mild reply.

For an academic year or two thereafter (time's main measure in small towns with large universities, even among the non-academic), he experimented, dutifully if less than enthusiastically, with various activities recommended for new retirees by the appropriate campus office: joined an alumni tour group for a week's visit to London; tried to interest himself in such hobbies (he'd never had a hobby) as contract bridge and Elderhosteling; volunteered briefly (the retirement-office people were big on volunteering) in a Head Start program designed to help black inner-city youngsters overcome their academic disadvantages, but directed locally, *faute de pis,* at their poor white Appalachian counterparts. But London overwhelmed and the game of bridge intimidated him; "at his age" he took no pleasure in learning complicated things from scratch and going places with groups of strangers. And while he pitied the young hillbilly left-behinds, he had no knack for motivating them to attempt what they themselves evinced little interest in. By the end of his first retirement year he looked forward to none of those activities. Midway through his second he dropped them all and settled into a routine of reading front to back the *Centre Daily* and *New York Times* through breakfast and beyond, then going for an extended walk if weather permitted or pottering about the condo if it didn't; perhaps lunching in town (sometimes with ex-colleagues), doing afternoon errands, or strolling the vast campus a bit. At five, back at the condo, he took a glass of red wine on his small screened porch or before the gas fireplace, then sipped another while preparing and eating his simple dinner. And finally—unless there was some interesting public lecture or other university event on the calendar—he settled down among his parents' furniture in his tidy living room to entertain himself with magazine or library book, television or desktop computer.

Was he bored? Of course he was, now and then, though not acutely. Anyhow, he was accustomed to the feeling and didn't much mind it; wasn't overly bored by boredom. Depressed? He had his ups and downs, neither of much amplitude; was and had prevailingly been of placid, equable disposition. Lonesome? Not especially, nor reclusive either, just solitary. On any stroll or shopping errand, he would likely exchange cordialities with one or more familiars; if he had no real friends, he had old acquaintances aplenty, some dating back to kindergarten. Happy? Not particularly, but (as afore-established) not unhappy either: more or less content.

And so we find him—one fine mid-May afternoon shortly after the university's spring commencement, when the wholesale exodus of tens of thousands of students leaves the town and campus spookily evacuated until various summer programs kick in—driving his high-mileage chalk-white Toyota Corolla out toward a nearby shopping plaza after lunch, with the aim of picking up a few groceries and maybe a DVD to spectate over the next two evenings, there being nothing listed in the *TV Guide* of much interest to him. Who can say why, upon reaching the plaza, he canceled his turn signal and drove on past the entrance? Perhaps with the object of replenishing his wine rack first, at the state liquor dispensary a bit farther on? Reaching it, he slowed and resignaled, but once again didn't stop; found himself continuing north another dozen miles through assorted hill and valley villages until the state two-laner T-boned into Interstate 80, which from that point crosses central Pennsylvania, east to New York City and west to Ohio and beyond. On some impulse beyond his articulating, he turned west, set the Corolla's cruise control to (as it happened) approximately the speed matching his age, and, under a fair-weather cumulus-clouded sky, steered through Allegheny hills green with young deciduous leaves, old hemlocks, and newly sprouting farm fields, without wondering (as if on cruise control himself) where he was going or why, or for that matter who it was, exactly, at the wheel.

Not having planned an extended drive, he hadn't topped off the car's fuel tank. Already by exit 22 (Snow Shoe), just a couple of dozen miles along the interstate, its gauge showed barely enough gas remaining to get him back home. He registered that datum, but drove on. He had with him no water bottle or other refreshment, and felt some thirst, but drove on. Not far from where I-80 crosses the winding headwaters of the Susquehanna's West Branch—which loops north and east from there up to Williamsport before commencing its long run south past Harrisburg and down to Chesapeake Bay—in a forested stretch between exits for Clearfield and Du Bois, the Corolla's four-cylinder engine sputtered dry. Fortunately, there was scant traffic just then on that stretch of highway; moreover, he happened to be on a downgrade, with enough momentum to give him ample time to steer out of the traffic lanes without obliging others to slow down or swing out to pass. His foot still uselessly on the accelerator of the stalled engine, he coasted down the wide shoulder until the slope bottomed out and the Corolla rolled to a stop without his having pressed the brake pedal. So as not to endanger vehicles approaching from behind, he activated the hazard flasher, but didn't bother to shift to Park or switch off the ignition. From the roadside woods a lean brown rabbit ran onto the highway shoulder just before him. It paused, sat up on its hind legs, regarded the unmoving vehicle, and scuttled back.

Now I'm in for it, one imagines Phil Blank supposing as he sits there conjuring scenarios of interrogation by the state Highway Patrol: questions to which he can no more anticipate his response, if any, than he could say just who the "I" is who's "in for it": the creature named by the name on his Commonwealth of Pennsylvania driver's license and the Toyota's registration card, who already now needs to pee, but can't decide whether to exit his car and discreetly wet the ground on its passenger side or simply to stay put and, sooner or later, wet himself. In short, to *do* nothing—not unlock the car doors or lower its driver-side window or speak or even turn his head when the patrol person or whoever eventually appears. To take no action beyond Taking No Action, and let whatever might happen, happen.

PART THREE: THE THIRD PERSON

Fred "I've Been Told" Story: Question, please?

"Self-Appointed Sidekick" Izzy-the-Teller: Yes?

F. "I.B.T." S.: So what happened next?

"S.-A.S.K." I.-t.-T.: Next? Nothing.

Fred: Whatcha mean, nothing? *Something* has to happen next! Something *always* happens next!

Izzy: Nope.

Hitherto Unmentioned Female Third Person [speaking from rear seat of Herocycle: a mid-fortyish, probably once-slender woman, she, bespectacled and bright-serious of expression, clothed in gray sweatshirt, blue jeans, and once-white walking shoes, straight black hair cut short in helmet style]: May I clarify? In Real Life, as it's called, something always happens next: the unlikely pants-wetting, the Highway Patrol car, the sister alarmed that her brother's gone missing, various embarrassing and troublesome consequences for poor-fuck Phil—whatever. In Fiction, on the other hand, that's not the case: Phil's *story* ends when it's finished, and its ending isn't necessarily conterminous in either direction with his imaginable lifespan.

I.: You got that right, ma'am: Next page would be blank, if there were one. Which there isn't.

F.: Much obliged for the fill-in. And who might *you* be, by the way?

H.U.F.T.P.: Third wheel on this Mythmobile, maybe? Go figure. Question for Teller?

I.: Be my guest—though I've a hunch it's we who're yours.

T.P. [waving off that consideration and tapping sheaf of manuscript pages in left hand]: Two questions, come to think of it. First off, in the lead-in to "_____'s Story" you declared, and I quote *[finds relevant page in aforementioned sheaf]:* "A story that'll serve as Fred's and mine here in Part Two of "A Story's Story" happens to be that of _____ . . ." But I, for one, don't see the connection. Your Phil Blank was never capital-A Anybody: His life and career were just a series of halfhearted attempts to address the teasing imperative of his name, if I may so put it. Pathetic, maybe, but hardly heroic. Fred here, on the contrary—if I may call you that, sir?

F.: Shrug.

T.P.: Fred's career has been an unparalleled success worldwide for going on three millennia . . .

F.: So I've been told.

T.P.: No culture in sight without some version of you! And your sidekick Izzy-the-Teller here's no Phil Blank either. Granted *[brandishes paper-sheaf],* he and/or his capital-A Author have filled blank pages by the ream with the words and sentences of made-up stories, some of which've been more successful than others, shall we say, with critics and reviewers and us Mere Readers—

I.: Why, thankee there, ma'm'selle. And welcome aboard, as always.

F. [to T.P.]: So *that's* who you are! Okay, I get your "third wheel" thing.

T.P. [to both]: What *I* don't get is how "_____'s Story" is you-guys' story. That's my First Question.

F. [to Isidore]: Hey, I don't get that either, Iz, come to think of it.

I.: First Question perpended. Be it noted, by the way, that Feckless Phil there didn't *decide* to do nothing: His story ends with his *inability* to decide. You had another question, I believe you said?

T.P.: Did and do. We Mere Readers had expected that once your so-called Ground Situation was established and this so-called Dramatic Vehicle got under way, plot complications would promptly follow, in the form of capital-O Obstacles and capital-A Adversaries, you know? But simply barreling westward like this down a straight flat narrative road is mere Action; it gets us nowhere, capital-P Plotwise. I'm reminded of the distinction in classical physics between Effort and Work: We're chugging along, but nothing's getting *done.* So my Second Question is, What gives?

It seemed to Fred that he'd heard of those distinctions—Action versus Plot, Effort versus Work—somewhere or other a long while back. They struck him as reasonable, and having no reply to their passenger-or-host's objection, he considered pulling off the road and parking the Herocycle/Mythmobile while the three of them discussed the matter. Maybe imperturbable Izzy had another six-pack stashed somewhere, to lubricate the discussion? Just then, however—as if their vehicle itself were given pause by Ms. Mere Reader's observation—its engine balked and quit, as had Phil Blank's Corolla's, and like that identity-challenged fellow, they coasted to a halt.

But Izzy the Teller, far from sharing Fred's concern and Reader's puzzlement, seemed merely amused. With a left-handed palm-up gesture at their situation, "*Voilà,*" he said to the pair of them. "Any further questions?"

"Not till I've thought through these ones," said Fred with a frown. "Seems to me we're as out of gas as poor-fart Phil there."

Beaming, Izzy nodded and *voilà*'d his left hand again.

"What I suppose," then supposed Mere Reader from the

seat behind them, "is that Izzy told us the Phil Blank story while we rattled westward just to fill the blank till the Next Thing happens—*and* to get another story told, in the same spirit as Fred's racking up the DV mileage just for the satisfaction of being on the move again."

Fred: That about says it, for me anyhow.

Izzy: Smiles knowingly while waiting for Third Person to continue.

F.: That's a line of dialogue?

I.: Why not? If Miz Fellow Traveler here can speak the words "_____'s Story," as she managed to do twice or thrice a few pages back, then I reckon *I* can speak third-person stage directions. *[To F.T.P. Mere Reader (speaking the words "To F.T.P. Mere Reader"):]* You were saying?

In narrative format again, "*Asking,* actually," that personage replied. "Your left-handed response to my First Question, I take it, is that the Herocycle's running out of gas like Phil Blank's Corolla just as I posed my *Second* Question effectively answers my First, namely: In what sense does *his* story serve as Fred's-and-yours?"

Applauded Izzy, "A two-handed *voilà encore!*"

But "Now just wait a mothering minute," objected Fred. "Maybe he and we both eventually ran dry, but up till then (as has been noted) our stories are different tales for sure. Phil's fate might resemble Izzy's, in his role as my tuckered-out Teller *du jour;* if so, tough titty for him, and better luck next time out. But it sure as shootin's not *my* story. Am I right, Miz Mere?"

Declared Izzy before that entity could reply, "You're right as far as you go, chum—but as far as you go is right here. Point being that unless we fall by the wayside earlier on, right here's where we all end up: by the wayside. What's more—"

Eagerly interrupted here Mere Reader, "What's more, Fred dear, as I'm just now beginning to appreciate, our ambidextrous Izzy might be getting more work done with those left-handed *voilàs* of his than we've been giving him credit for."

F.: Yeah? How's that?

"*Fred's Self-Appointed Sidekick beams,*" here beamed that very fellow, "and with his *right* hand"—which now held, instead of the Swiss Army knife, a capped fountain pen—"bids our keen-eyed, not-so-Mere Reader to say on."

Adjusting with one forefinger a lick of her helmeted hair, "Yes, well: Speaking of herself in third person like Maestro Izzy, what she's just now remembering is that this buggy—which, by the way, since I'm its Wheel Three, I presume you guys to be Wheels One and Two of, in whatever order?—that this buggy, I was saying, isn't just the so-called Herocycle: It's also Fred I've-Been-Told's story's Dramatic Vehicle, right? As was established back in what we're calling retrospectively Part One, and unlike Phil Blank's Corolla in Part Two, which was just a lowercase vehicle."

F. & I. [more or less in unison]: Ergo?

"Ergo, guys, when *ours* ran out of gas just as I happened to be complaining in my Second Question that this I.B.T. tale is overdue for a capital-C Complication to turn the screws on its capital-C Conflict and advance its ditto-P Plot, what that Arresting Vehicular Coincidence amounts to—what we have on our narrative/dramaturgical hands right here right now—is nothing less than dot dot dot . . ."

"By George!" cried Fred. "A bona fide, gen-you-wine Complication!"

"Georg*ina,*" corrected now-demure-but-not-displeased-with-herself Ms. Reader, this time adjusting her rimless specs. "Just doing my job, fellows."

"And doing it well indeed," commended wire-rimmed Izzy.

Heartily agreed old Fred, "Good show!" And to his front-seat-mate then, "So?"

"So let Mademoiselle *Lectrice* read on," smoothly suggested that personage. "Next paragraph of this story, please, my dear? Followed by the next after that?"

"Uh, excuse me?" Looking around her rear seat, then the forward one, and the itemless landscape round about. "*What* next paragraph?"

"The one you just recited to us'll do, I suppose, that went *Uh, excuse me,* et cet? Followed by this one that *I'm* speaking and you're just now reading. On with our story, s.v.p.?"

Unless his head-nodding was a senior moment, Protagonist Fred seemed to find this proposal agreeable. Ms. Reader Georgina, on the contrary—having retrieved that earlier-flourished script-sheaf from under her butt, where she'd secured it back when their vehicle was speeding along, and fumbling now through its latter pages—protested, "*What* story? *What* next paragraph? Last time I looked, this thing here ended with the end of '_____'s Story.' "

Maybe look again, suggested Izzy. She having so done, "Okay," Ms. puzzled G. acknowledged, "so now it ends with my asking you what in fact I was just about to ask you: *How can I read what hasn't been written down yet?* What's going on here?"

"Seems to Fred and me you're doing just fine." But he offered her the capped fountain pen. "Care to give this gizmo a try?"

His idea of a joke? she challenged him—her speech, for a change, paraphrased instead of quoted directly. In the first place, "Izzy," not she, was the self-declared Teller of this so-called tale; let the cobbler stick to his last! And in the second place, even if she were inclined to take over his job, which she most decidedly was not, these manuscript pages (although they now extended as if magically to the parenthesis in progress) were written on both sides of each sheet, leaving not a blank scrap for her to write on—or, come to think of it, for him or anybody else to write on! "Hey, now . . . ?"

"Complications left and right!" Fred marveled. "Seems to me the lady has a point there, Iz. And that this out-of-gas story of ours is moving right along, even though we-all aren't. Who's driving?"

Acknowledged unruffled Isidore, "A point she'd have, friend, were't not that the pair of you seem to've forgotten our little Narrative-Point-of-View review back in Part Two. Wherein, be ye twain reminded, 'twas pointed out that while this 'I've Been Told' story both *is* Fred and is *about* Fred, its Teller this time around is Yours Truly—most explicitly so in Part Two, but at least arguably so in Parts One and Three as well, Teller having merely shifted narrative POVs between acts like a quick-change artist."

"Excuse me?" here objected bright-eyed but still mystified Georgina-the-Reader, who'd been listening attentively to this spiel, her chin resting on the back of her hands, which rested in turn on the inexorably lengthening script, itself resting now atop the front seatback. "It seems to *this* Mere Reader—"

"And right she is again," affirmed Izzy. What perhaps (with her indulgence) wanted clarification, he went on, was the term *Teller,* which comprises more than one aspect. For just as a Story is not its Teller ("Fred's not Izzy, is he?"), so also its Teller—in the sense of its Narrator, anyhow—is not its Author, their job descriptions being quite different even when, as here and there happens, Author and Narrator are two functions of the same functionary, or pretend so to be. Teller-in-the-sense-of-Author *invents* and renders into language either the story itself—its characters, setting, action, plot, and theme—or (as in present instance) some new version of a pre-existing story. Teller-in-the-sense-of-Narrator then delivers Author's invention—renders his rendition, so to speak—whether as a story character himself, like Present Speaker, or as a more or less disembodied narrative voice. Or, for that matter, as an *embodied* narrative voice, back in oral-tradition days when tales were literally told or sung, passed along from bard to bard instead of printed for silent perusal by individual Georginas.

"Sigh," sighed Fred. "Those were the days."

"Not for us quote *individual Georginas* they weren't," objected she. "You can *'Sigh,' sighed Fred* all you want, but for us Mere Readers *these* are the days: Go at our own pace! Reread any passage we particularly enjoy or maybe don't quite understand. Skip ahead or check back; start or stop or hit Pause anywhere and anywhen we damn please—couldn't do that back there with Homer and Company! But we're off the subject, guys, which is, and I quote *[reads aloud from current last lines of script]:* 'Reads aloud from current last lines of script: *Is Izzy our Author, or isn't he?*' Who's writing this pedantical crapola? Is there a fourth wheel on this wagon?"

"Plus, *How do we get the sumbitch rolling, Perfessor?* adds Old-Fart Fred," adds Etc., tapping his bony chest. "How do we get *me* rolling?"

Instead of replying directly to those questions, imperturbable Izzy brandished again that afore-flourished fountain pen. "Notice it's capped, chaps: That's its *point,* one could say. Here fished forth to *make* the point that I myself am no more than Fred's willy-nilly teller *du jour,* not his author nor yours nor my own. Who our Author is, who knoweth? Not we Mere Fictional Characters! All *we* know is that while quote *real* people in the quote *real* world may do things out of their more-or-less-free will, all we MFCs have is the semblance thereof, while in fact we do precisely what Mister/Miz Author seeth fit to write that we do. Even Ms. Reader, once she entered this tale as its Georgina-the-Mere-Reader character, checked her own volition at the door: She may *think* she can exit our script anytime she wishes, but if she does, it's because Author decided to send her packing. *End of speech,* it says here."

She should be so lucky, commented the referred-to MFC—who, however (she went on to say), like the story she'd made the mistake of getting involved in, was going nowhere, at least not until she had an Isidorean answer to Fred's question: How do we get this out-of-gas jalopy up and running? If, as appeared to be the case, their real magical weapon/tool/whatever was not Izzy's Swiss Army knife but Author's uncapped pen, and if (as would appear to follow) the Mythmobile's ultimate fuel was the Ink of Inspiration, so to speak, then how do we get that pen filled and flowing—or, to change metaphoric implements, how put some fresh lead in the old pencil? Are we not back where we started in Part One, at the Place Where Three Roads Diverge, awaiting some refueled Dramatic Vehicle?

With the smile of one who knows something his questioners don't (or who would be seen as such), Izzy set down the manuscript, pocketed that pen, and turned up his palms. The sun, which would have long since set had Author not apparently lost track of time, resumed its setting. O.-F. Fred turned his What Now? visage from one to the other of his cycle-mates—of whom only determined and resourceful Georgina, it would appear, had the presence of mind to reach over the front seatback at this point, fetch up the script, move its top page (the most recently read, which at the time had ended with her saying, "*End of speech,* it says here," but now extended through the present paragraph) to the bottom, as she and Izzy in turn had done with the pages they'd read before it, and thereby expose to view the "new" page beneath, subheaded "4. The Fourth Wheel." From which, she being after all our Reader, in the belated sunset's long last light, she read aloud what follows this colon:

4. THE FOURTH WHEEL

Author speaking, more-than-patient Reader, in order to declare—at the risk of seeming uncooperative or coy—that it matters not a whit to "Fred" 's story who its author is, as long as the job gets done. Which is (as "Izzy" pointed out a while back at some length indeed) to "craft" the thing, as they say nowadays: to put it through its dramaturgical paces, goose it along through serial/incremental complications to its climax and denouement, possibly enlightening but at least *entertaining* you: "holding [your] attention," says the dictionary, between your presumably more mattersome affairs. Whether I've so done and am so doing isn't for me to judge—except when I role-shift from Author to Reader-of-what-I've-authored,* about which I confess my feelings to be mixed.

* Just as I've shifted here, with "Izzy" 's indulgence, from Author to Teller *du soir* (it being now evening) of "Fred" 's Part Four.

Who wouldn't rather read a straight-on *story*-story, involving colorful characters doing interesting things in a "dramatic" situation, instead of yet another peekaboo story-about-storying? Why not one in which "Fred," for example—whether or not he may be said to represent the timeless, ubiquitous Myth of the Wandering Hero—is first and foremost a palpable presence on the page? A prevailingly likable, though curmudgeonish, once-upon-a-time super-achiever, say, now on his next-to-last legs: an ex-hard-driving CEO, maybe, or even—why not?—an ex-president of the USA (quite a few of *those* around nowadays), who did world-altering things while in office and is chafing so at the relative impotency of retirement (especially as he abhors and fears his incumbent successor) that he concocts a last-hurrah scheme, crazy-sounding but just possibly bring-offable, to (etc.)? This with the aid of "Izzy," as his career-long adviser and former White House chief of staff likes to be called: a now-also-geriatric master manipulator who, in their joint prime, virtually told "Fred" what to say and do (or, rather, how most effectively to say and do it, Fred himself being nobody's puppet), and who not only, like his boss/colleague/advisee, much misses his role in the wings and prompter's booth of power, but finds Fred's proposed spin on what was actually *Izzy's* last-hurrah plan so almost certainly disastrous that he resolves for the nation's and the world's sake to quietly derail while appearing to copilot it, excuse the split infinitive and mixed metaphor?

Et cetera? And as for "Georgina" . . . but forget it, Reader: The above-sketched is Another Story, which you're free to shift roles and take a shot at authoring yourself, so to speak, if something like that's what you'd rather read than this. Having borne with me, however, while I fetched that trio and their formerly three-wheeled whatchacallum from the Place Where Three Roads Meet or Diverge, depending, through the three episodes leading to their apparent present impasse, permit me to declare (what Iz seems to have been quite aware of and Georgina to have come to realize) that while their Dramatic Vehicle has been stalled for many a script page now, "Fred" himself (I mean this I've-Been-Told Story's story) has been moving right along.

It is, in fact, all but told. For was it not you yourself —I mean, of course, Georgina the Mere but Sharp-Eyed Reader—who pointed out that her sudden appearance (in Part Three: The Third Person) in order to question the relevance of "_____'s Story" was itself a complication of *Fred's* story? And that her subsequently invoking the distinction between Action and Plot, together with her observation that merely chugging westward was not equivalent to Getting Somewhere, was the next complication after that, leading as it did to the Herocycle's immediate out-sputtering and the threesome's (apparent) ongoing impasse, et cetera, et cetera, right through Izzy's revelation of—rather, his leading Georgina to discover for herself—the ever-incrementing nature of their script, even unto the still-moving point of Author's pen? As tidy a series of Complications as ever rode the up escalator toward Finale! There remains only the business of Climax, Denouement, and Wrap-Up to complete the classical curve of dramatic action and Author's self-imposed assignment—a task just at this point interrupted, he imagines, by impassioned female grunts and groans from the rear seat of the Dramatic Vehicle: "Yes. Yes! *Yes!*" Their source is our Regina (the former Georgina, her name here and now changed by authorial fiat, she being the very Queen of Readers), so excited by the realization that their impasse has been only apparent—that in dramaturgical fact they've been not merely expending Energy but accomplishing Work—that to her happy embarrassment she finds herself climaxing indeed: "*Yes!*"

Izzy winks at Fred and with a gesture invites the old warhorse into the back seat with their so-aroused mare. But Author objects to Story's ever taking the back seat in its own Dramatic Vehicle: Instead, with a few strokes of his pen he transports transported Regina into the buggy's *front* seat with Fred and shifts Izzy-the-Sometime-Teller into the rear beside his authorial self.

"*Yesyesyes!*" moans Regina (an ejaculation not easily moaned, but she manages it), and makes to place Fred's gnarled but still handy right hand where her gnarl-free left has been busying itself. Waggish Izzy nudges Author and (behind his own right hand) suggests, "Her mons veneris for his Mysterious Hilltop Consummation? Let's do it!"

But Author decides to have Fred content himself with declaring to his ardent seat-mate that while her invitation to literal intercourse between Story and Reader flatters and honors him, he in turn honors and respects both her and his patient family back yonder, who have put up with and loyally supported him through the mattersome chapters of his Regnancy, Fall from Favor, and Departure from the City—yea, even unto his fast-approaching Mysterious End. Too grateful is he to all hands to dishonor them and himself as well with Protagonistic infidelity at this late stage of their joint story (as an early Complication, he allows, it might have been interesting indeed—but that would've been Another Story).

"*Ah!* Ah! Ah." So moved is Regina by Fred's profession of love for and loyalty to his household (R. is, after all, along with her other adjectives, the *Faithful* Reader), she finds herself once more auto-orgasming: Climax enough, Author here submits, for this story's story. Sometime-Teller Izzy, while skeptical of that submission, obligingly offers the so-moved Third Person, over the seatback, his own hand for her possible employment. Regina gives him a not-unfriendly mind-your-own-business look—as much as to say, "It's *stories* that turn me on, buster, not their tellers or authors"—and returns her admiring attention to our Hero.

Whom, however, she discovers to be no longer in the seat beside her; nor has he shifted to the rear with his Enablers. The Mythmobile's driver's door is open; the driver himself, it would appear, has vanished into the circumambient dark. Her hand still in place but no longer busy, "Fred?" the lady calls plaintively. "Freddie?"

As if from out of sight on the road's far side, "Gotta go now, ma'am," that old fellow's voice comes back. "Much obliged for the lift, guys. See you around. Maybe."

"*Fre-ed?!*"

But she understands the fitness of it, does our savvy Reader, sweetly disappointed but dramaturgically fulfilled; the fitness too of her not knowing whither trudgeth her aged admiree: back homeward or farther westward, none knows where. Upon that matter, should they discuss it, she and Izzy will disagree, Regina preferring to imagine Fred's ultimate Consummation in the bosom of his family, in the heart of their once-excellent city, Isidore inclining to a more mysterious, indeed unknown and unknowable finale somewhere out yonder—indeed, perhaps not even *down* the road after all, but *off* it: somewhere trackless, out beyond that far shoulder whence last we heard his voice.

Author himself refrains from tipping the scales either

way. Enough, in his opinion, to have Regina recollect, aloud, that the Ur-Mythic script includes the possibility of our Hero's being, at the end, not really dead, but rather transmigrated to some Elsewhere—whence, in time, he will return . . .

"Isn't that so?" she demands of us back-seaters—and, without waiting for our opinion, calls fretfully across to where she last heard his voice: "Freddie? Isn't it so, hon? That we'll meet again someday, somewhere?"

To which, from a remove more distant than before, one barely hears his ancient voice reply (by Regina's hopeful account), "*So I've been told.*"

Or perhaps (as Izzy will prefer to tell it), "*So: I've been told.*"

III

AS I WAS SAYING . . .

TAPE 1

. . . dear Listener, before Grace noticed we'd forgotten to push the Record button on Junior's machine: This portion of the oral history of Manfred Dickson's famous novel-trilogy—

"Better say Dickson *Senior's* trilogy, Aggie. Manny Senior's *infamous* trilogy."

—Manfred F. Dickson Senior's once-notorious and controversial but now virtually forgotten masterwork, *The Fates,* okay? This unofficial contribution to the project (as I was saying, until Thelma interrupted me) will be the collective recollections of the Mason sisters, as recorded in our Bernbridge Manor apartments in Bernbridge, Maryland, on New Year's Eve 1999.

"Three burned-out former floozies in the Burnt-Bridge Old Farts' Home."

Have it your way, Thelm. These interruptions, I was saying, are courtesy of our irrepressible sister Thelma—

"Thalia the Unrepressed to you folks out there in Listener Land: a still-frisky seventy-pluser who likes to tweak her dear doddering elders."

Kid Sister Thelma/Thalia, all of eighteen months younger than the rest of us . . .

Which is to say, folks, just a tad younger than my twin sister Agatha—our Lead-Off Narrator, you might say—and her *twin sister Grace (temporarily speaking), who'll transcribe these off-the-record recordings and add her two cents' worth as we go along. Aggie in roman type, Thelma in quotes, and me in italics ought to keep things clear. You were saying, Ag?*

. . . Sister Thelma/Thalia, I was saying: still the sharp-tongued wiseass brat of our golden girlhood.

"Excuse me, sis: I hope and believe I have my head on straight, but my ass was never my wisest part."

Amen to that, for the three of us. Always remembering, however, girls, that once upon a time it was these tushies of ours that paid our way through college.

And made us secretly famous, Listener—as it were? Unbeknownst to any except ourselves and a certain . . . Señor Senior, shall we call him?

"If only we *could* call up old Manny, who made the Mason sisters . . . what? Anonymously famous? Temporarily immortal?"

As maybe we'll be again, less anonymously and temporarily, if Manny Junior has his way.

"Or if we have *our* way with Junior."

[Chuckles]

Imagine *that,* now: a Three-Way with that uptight little putz! Talk about *wise!*

Aggie's pun on Y's *lost in transcription, Listener, as it will be in translation like*wise *(excuse me) if "Junior" 's critical study of his once-fairly-famous dad ever gets written, published, and translated into languages other than English. And hey, girls, we're piling up inside jokes and allusions at such a clip that this oral history of ours is going to need footnotes and commentaries.*

Leave those to Herr Doktor Professor Junior: It's what prissies like him are *for,* right? He wants oral, we'll give him oral.

"Plus vaginal and anal! The old Mason-Dixon Three-Way!"

You wish. But Gracie's got a point there: We probably ought to start over.

Would that we could. From scratch.

"As in You scratch mine and I'll scratch yours?"

Scratch the interruptions, Thal, or we'll never get our effing story told.

"Our Effing Story . . ."

As I was saying, people—or've been *trying* to get said from Square One? Better yet, Grace: *You* fill the folks in, orally or otherwise, and then we'll get on with our three-part harmony. Tell 'em where we're coming from, and why.

"And where all our coming went, and why all those Y's in Manny's *Fates . . .*"

Speaking of Y's, guys—Y's-guys?—Y2K's about to hit Times Square, and how many turn-of-the-millenniums do we Once-and-Future Immortals get to raise a glass to? So be a good sis and pop us some bubbly, Thal, while Aggie fetches the flutes and I slug a fresh tape into Junior's gizmo—

"Now *that* sounds like fun."

—and tomorrow we'll start over.

"Hah. Spare me."

What *I* suggest, Grace, is that instead of us starting a new tape now, you write up some kind of introduction to this big-deal oral history—

"Right on, Agatha. Grace has always been the family scribbler, see, Listener: term papers for the three of us back in college days; bookkeeping ledgers for our little business; suggestions and corrections for Manny's scripts. Manny-scripts? Not to mention *diaries . . .*"

Not to mention certain better-she-hadn't-kept-'em diaries. But as I was saying: Let's clink glasses now, and then at Happy Hour tomorrow Grace'll read her scribbles and we'll take it from there: Lambda Upsilon! Dining at the Y! The works!

You'll do the reading, Aggie. I just cook the books.

[Knowing chuckles. Pop of champagne cork. Strains of Auld Lang Syne *from TV coverage of millennial New Year's Eve festivities.]*

So: To inspiration?

"We all know what *that* means. Bottoms up!"

[More chuckles. Clink of glasses.]

Here's to us, then.

"To us."

Us.

And now it's tomorrow already, everybody—specifically, half an hour and one glass of Mumm Brut into January 1, 2000, which astronomer types tell us isn't really *the new millennium's kickoff, but never mind those party poopers—and no need for a new tape yet, 'cause there's room enough left on this one to explain that a letter recently arrived at Bernbridge Manor addressed to* Ms. Grace Mason [Forester] *(my former married name set like that in brackets) and letterheaded* Arundel University, *which used to be Arundel* State *University, which used to be Arundel State* College, *which used to be Arundel State* Teachers *College when Agatha and Thelma and I worked our butts off, so to speak, to earn our degrees there back in the fifties. To my less-than-total surprise—and Aggie's and "Thalia"'s when I passed the thing around—it was a* very *lengthy letter of introduction from one Dr. Manfred F. Dickson Jr., Ph.D., professor of social history at Arundel U. and son of "the undeservedly neglected writer of the same name," whom he understood my sisters and me to have known in his father's "formative years." Perhaps we had heard, the letter went on, that nearby Mason-Dixon University (a considerably more upscale operation, Listener, than our ASTC/ASC/ASU/AU)—Manfred Senior's alma mater, where he'd later taught for a few years while writing the first and second volumes of* The Fates, *and where Manfred Junior had been born and raised until his parents split and the ruckus over those books got his old man sacked—was belatedly and cautiously reappreciating their notorious alumnus, as were some literary historians, and had proposed to name a new classroom building, or at least one of its seminar rooms, in his honor. Not surprisingly, even the more modest of these proposals was meeting with resistance from conservative trustees of the university. The letter writer himself, he would have me know, much respected his father's work despite its "perhaps excessive ribaldry"; in the 1960s, after all, it had been regarded in some quarters as a comic/erotic epic: John Dos Passos's* U.S.A. *with sex, humor, and "mythopoeic fantasy"; Henry Miller's* Tropics *in the Age of Aquarius; "an in-*

valuable sociohistorical record of mid-century America." He welcomed any renewed public controversy on the subject, Junior declared, despite the attendant associations with his parents' divorce, his mother's lifelong resentments, and his father's pitiable final years, inasmuch as he himself was at work on a three-volume historical/critical/biographical study of Manfred Senior's life and times, from his Roosevelt-era boyhood and eventual discovery of his vocation after several false starts, through the "mature" period of his fixation on the Heroic Cycle and his composition of the Fates *trilogy between 1957 and 1963—the Eisenhower-Kennedy era of America's Korean and Vietnam wars and the U.S.-Soviet Cold War and space race—to his obscure end in the rebellious, countercultural high 1960s. Along the way, he declared, he hoped to "address and perhaps even resolve" such "cardinal mysteries of Dickson scholarship" as the author's obsession with* threes *in general and Y's in particular: obsessions that, together with the notorious Myth of the Wandering Hero, "bind the three otherwise disparate novels into a trilogy." And who, exactly, were the enigmatic "Gracious Masons, who lent me their ears," to whom the monumental work is cryptically thus dedicated (instead of to its author's long-suffering spouse, the letter writer's mother, "who surely deserved that honor")?*

Et cetera, blah blah blah.

It was in pursuit of this latter question, Dr. Dickson's letter went on (and on and on), that his attention had lately been brought to a more recent work of "experimental" fiction: a novella-length piece called Wye, *by one C. Ella Mason (an author previously unknown to him), featured in the Spring 1999 issue of his (and our) university's literary quarterly,* The Arundel Review. *Ms. Mason's story (as he presumed I knew, its author happening to be my daughter) is a roman à clef concerning the dismissal in 1974 of two respected faculty members of the "Annapolis School for Girls" (a transparent alias for the Severn Day School, Listener, where Aggie and I so loved our years of teaching) on the grounds that twenty years earlier they had worked as prostitutes to earn their tuition at "Wye College," in the course of which enterprise they had met, serviced, and, it seems, inspired a budding young writer named "Fred," of whom more presently.*

The teachers in question are a long-standing member of the "ASG" English Department named "Mrs. Woodsman" and her sister, a more recently hired theater and gymnastics coach; the scandal of their past comes to light when the former's husband discovers, in 1973, diaries kept by his wife from the late 1940s, before their marriage, through the following decade (in the course of which they had wed and bred) and into the early 1960s. They reveal to him not only his wife's shocking premarital past, of which he was altogether unaware, but also that in the seven years from 1955 to 1962 she had "maintained a relationship" (also unknown to him) with the aforementioned "Fred," who by then had blossomed into the up-and-coming avant-garde novelist "Frederick Manson": a period extending from the conception of his controversial erotic trilogy The Graces *through its initial publication and its author's termination from the faculty of "Wye College," whereto he had returned as writer-in-residence. The scandalized husband—a conservative country-club-Republican dealer in suburban D.C. commercial real estate named "Ed Woodsman"—successfully presses for divorce and custody of the couple's two late-teenage children despite his mate's honest protestations that her past is past; that throughout her marriage she has been an exemplary wife and mother; that her "relationship" with Adjunct Professor "Manson" had been exclusively editorial, assisting him with the research and composition of his subsequently world-famous and unjustly maligned masterwork, which in her admittedly subjective opinion bade to be to the century's second half what James Joyce's* Ulysses *(similarly banned as "obscene" until District Court Judge John M. Woolsey's landmark 1933 ruling to the contrary) was to its first. In sum, that she is reprehensible only in having kept from her husband her early sexual history and her subsequent, altogether* nonsexual *connection with "Frederick Manson," on the grounds that her dear dour spouse was incapable of understanding, much less of forgiving, those omissions.*

The family court judge (so went C. Ella Mason's Wye *novella, insofar as the letter writer could follow its story line through its off-putting postmodernist narrative devices) is unimpressed; likewise the headmistress and trustees of the Annapolis School for Girls, much as they value Mrs. Woodsman's long and distinguished service to that institution and her more recently appointed but comparably popular sister's as well (had they known about Aggie's activities between her college days and her Severn Day School appointment, Listener, there'd have been even more hell to pay!). The two women lose their jobs; the Annapolis School girls lose the best teachers they'll ever know; Mrs. Woodsman loses official custody of her children (but not their love, understanding, and sympathy, declares* Wye's *first-person narrator); she loses, too, her beloved-though-stuffy husband, first to the divorce that he insists upon, and soon after to his death by suicide, humiliated by the public scandal that he has himself precipitated. American literature, moreover, has by the present time of the* Wye *story long since lost to alcohol and despair the novelist "Frederick Manson," whose wife divorces* him *after his sacking from "Wye College." Concerning all which losses, the un-*

named narrator of Wye *asks of herself and of the reader (in a perhaps over-heavy closing-line pun),* Why?

While reserving judgment on the literary merits of Ms. Mason's lengthy short story, Manfred F. Dickson Jr.—the writer of this interminable letter of introduction, in case Listener has forgotten—declared himself to have been struck indeed by the obvious parallels between his father and "Frederick Manson," as between The Fates *and* "The Graces," *not to mention by the novella's echoing, in its title and in numerous elements of its construction, his father's signature preoccupation with, among other things, Y's. He had therefore promptly sought out its author, herself an adjunct professor of creative writing at a branch campus of the state university on Maryland's Eastern Shore; had introduced and identified himself; and had pressed her for details of the backstory of* Wye. *No doubt to protect her family's privacy, Ms. Mason—a quite pleasant woman about the same age as himself, he was pleased to report, who asked to be called Cindy—had insisted that her fiction was just that, pure fiction, although she readily acknowledged its echoing of themes and motifs from* The Fates. *She denied likewise any connection with or knowledge of the "Gracious Masons" of that trilogy's dedication, while admitting that the coincidence of her last name and those dedicatees' had been one inspiration of her novella. Unconvinced, but not wanting to press the subject against her wishes (Ms. Mason having been otherwise most hospitable to him, respectful of his father's literary accomplishment—to which she would not presume to compare her modest own—and particularly sympathetic in the matter of parental divorce and loss of sire), he then took it upon himself to computer-search her background and was not long in tracing her parentage, the essential similarities (but with important differences, Lis-*

tener) between Mr. and Mrs. "Ed Woodsman"'s history and that of Ned and Grace Mason Forester, and the latter's present address.

Having discovered which last (right under his nose, it turned out, in the Arundel U. alumni directory!), he earnestly hoped that she might grant him and "contemporary Dickson scholarship" the privilege of an extended interview on the details of her collaboration with his father: nothing indiscreet, she was to understand (the erotic, he declared, was "frankly not [his] cup of tea"), but perhaps the illumination of such questions as those mentioned earlier, and even of such relative details as why Clotho *(the first of the* Fates *novels, dealing with the hero's birth, boyhood, and discovery of his vocation) is emblemized on its title page and chapter headings with an inverted equiangular Y (i.e., ⅄), the second* (Lachesis, *the saga of the hero's serial labors) with the Y upright, and the third (*Atropos, *the story of his fall from favor and his mysterious end) with the emblem turned ninety degrees clockwise (-<).*

Might they, at her convenience, meet and talk? And if so, could she kindly supply him with driving directions to Bernbridge Manor, as he had tried in vain to find the town of Bernbridge both on his computer and on his AAA map of Maryland/Delaware/Virginia? . . .

TAPE 2

Okay: Press Record now, Gracie.

Already did that, Ag: The floor's yours.

"Not to mention bed and couch and any other available surface once upon a time, hey, Aggie?"

Can it, Thelm. You were saying, Ag?

. . . that meet the little weenie we did, Listener dear, and talked his maiden ears off for two hours straight yesterday afternoon. More than he bargained for!

"Or could handle. Did you see how he blanched when we solved his little riddles for him in the first half hour, and how he spent the next ninety minutes looking for a way to get his tushie out of here?"

Well: It wasn't really fair to spring the three of us on him when he was expecting just me. But who could resist?

His dad sure took it in stride, back in '48. But Manny Senior was a different story.

That he was: innocent, maybe, but eager to learn, and a very *quick study.*

And still in his teens then, Listener, don't forget. Whereas Manny Junior at age—what, mid-forties?—is plenty learned but still innocent, in our judgment, and self-programmed to stay that way. We'd bet he's never been laid in his life.

"By either sex, was Cindy's guess when she alerted Grace that we might be hearing from him."

All the same, it was *a bit much of us to pile on the Lambda Upsilon details, and offer to demonstrate . . .*

Like hell it was, Grace. If it's social history the guy's after, he should bring a camcorder instead of just audiotape, and let us show him what we're talking about! And I don't believe for a minute that he really *wants* three reels of us answering his scripted interview questions, now that he knows what he's gotten himself into. He was just politely hauling ass out of here.

"Bet he won't even come back to pick up this machine."

Yes, well, girls: Growing up as our *Manny's namesake and only child can't have been a picnic, right? With a mom who felt disgraced by her husband's notoriety and half suspected him of actually* doing *all the horny stuff he wrote about? Genius can be hard on the home folks.*

"Speaking of hard-ons . . ."

Would you quit that, Thal?

"Nope: In the interest of full and impartial social history, Listener needs to hear that when Aggie fetched out her famous three-in-one Ace of Clubs photo card from back in her 'modeling' days, let's say, old Junie-boy got a boner despite himself. Had to keep his clipboard on his lap to cover it."

Enough already about *Junie-boy:* Go back and start at our beginning now, Gracie, before we fill up this whole tape with chitchat. *Once upon a time there were these three little sisters*—stuff like that.

As I was about to say, Listener/Junior/Whoever: Once upon a World War Twotime there were three not-so-little Navy-brat teenage sisters in Annapolis EmDee, whose combat-officer dad survived the battles of Coral Sea and Leyte Gulf but not the accidental plane crash en route home after V-J Day, while his daughters were still in high school . . .

And whose widow became an acute depressive soon after—as our Thelma/Thalia did not, bless her, after *her* husband coughed his lungs out a few years ago, nor our Grace when hers unkindly dumped her back in the seventies—per Cindy-Ella's *Wye* story, but with important differences. Me, if I'd ever found myself a one-and-only and then lost him, I reckon I'd've gone Mom's route. But on with our story, Grace.

So we saw poor Ma as best we could through her get-me-out-of-here stage, which she abbreviated for us with a handful of sleeping pills enjoyed in the family Chevy idling with windows down in a closed garage while the three of us were out junior-senior promming . . .

"Thankee there, Ma, I guess, goddamn you, poor thing."

Whereafter we managed our own adolescence, as we'd pretty much been managing it already, and not remarkably well.

But we *did* by God manage it, folks, on Mom's Navy-widow pension, and decided on our own to go crosstown to ASTC and learn to be schoolteachers or accountants or something, if we could hack the tuition.

Which of course we couldn't, modest as it was, on our measly summer-job and babysitting wages—

"Until Socially Active Agatha, let's call her, happened to cross paths in a Georgetown club with a homely-but-rich boy from G. Washington U. who offered her ten for a blow-job, as I remember, or twenty for a backseat shag—good money in those days."

And said sister being already more round-heeled than well-heeled (she here readily admits), she shucked her last remaining virginity—namely, her amateur status—and came home neither with ten dollars nor with twenty, but with thirty, and an offer of more where that came from if she'd see fit to accommodate a couple of his classmates next time out.

Which she did, brave girl: half a dozen beer-guzzling undergrads, in the club basement of their frat house . . .

Serially, mind, instead of three at a crack, those being my early apprentice days.

"And came home this time with more than our next month's apartment rent, six times whatever being what it is, and rents back then being what *they* were."

And came home also with her mind made up that there *was her ticket to higher education: better-paying and less time-intensive than waitressing, and probably not* too *risky if she took the right hygienic/contraceptive precautions, steered clear of pimps and rough neighborhoods, and mainly worked the Washington/Baltimore/Annapolis college circuit.*

"Bit of social history here, if I may? Before and after the time we tell of, hookers in American college neighborhoods would've been a rarity. But in the nineteen-late-forties and fifties, the GI Bill flooded the campuses with older guys who'd been around the block: guys who mightn't have considered college without that free ticket, and whose military service had acquainted them with sex for hire."

Not that commercial-coital coeds like us were a standard feature of campus life even then, Listener, by any means. But we were imaginable, at least.

"Never mind imaginable, Aggie: We were *real.*"

It sure *felt* real, anyhow, for better or worse. You were saying, Grace?

. . . *that Aggie having blazed the trail, so to speak, and pointed the way to our B.A.s at ASTC, we followed her lead: Thelma less reluctantly than I, I guess, although she was still only seventeen—*

As opposed to *our* worldly-wise eighteen and a half . . .

—but I no less determinedly, since my heart was set on going to college.

"Gracie being the family scholar, as well as our record-keeper. And mind you, Listener: This particular seventeen-year-old had been around the block herself a few times already."

So we got down to business—

So to speak. And did we ever! Separately and together . . .

Never on our own campus, for propriety's sake, but working the student hangouts in Annapolis, Georgetown, and College Park—

Where the big state U. is, Listener, and the take per trick

was less than at the private colleges, but the customer-count was higher.

Mostly war vets, as established, but occasional tenderfeet as well—including first-timers, who were less intimidated by us nice coed types than they would've been by bona fide hookers. And mostly in the guys' cars (the ones who had *cars in those days) or off-campus rooms and apartments, but now and then in their fraternity houses.*

"Which brings us . . . *ta-da!* . . ."

To a certain spring Saturday in '48: Harry Truman winding up his term as FDR's successor and facing Thomas E. Dewey in the upcoming election, which we roundheel coeds weren't old enough yet to vote in. And just as we're finishing dinner and discussing where to peddle our merchandise that evening, and whether Arundel State Teachers T-shirts would be a turnoff or a come-hither on Wisconsin Avenue and environs, we get a call from a very *nervous-sounding lad up at Mason-Dixon U.: a turf we'd had our eyes on, it being the most prestigious hereabouts, but hadn't had a shot at yet.*

Here we go: Tell it, Gracie.

Introduced himself as Manfred Dickson, a freshman at MDU who was pledging Lambda Upsilon fraternity, known for its Hell Week hazing rituals—

"Such as olive races, where the pledges scramble naked through the house on all fours with olives in their ass-cracks while getting whacked on the butt with pledge paddles by their upperclass brothers, and whoever drops his olive has to eat it? Yuck."

And their famous scavenger hunt, where the poor fucks draw lots for such tasks as hauling up into Pennsylvania in the middle of the night to steal road signs for the towns of Bird-in-Hand, Intercourse, Paradise, and Blue Ball . . .

Or, in Pledge Dickson's case, producing for the brothers' pleasure a woman or women prepared to satisfy for a reasonable fee the carnal appetites of the entire chapter house: a task that he'd've flunked cold, he said, if one of the guys hadn't happened to be an ex-Marine junior-year transfer from the D.C. area who'd gotten our phone number from a Naval Academy plebe bar down our way, where we were sort of famous. And hey, he wanted to know: Didn't I think it meant something, quote-unquote, that my name was Mason and his was Dickson and our paths were fated to cross at Mason-Dixon U.? If, that is, we would please please PLEASE rescue his ass by letting one of his car-owning brothers pick us up pronto and fetch us to Lambda Ups for just a couple of hours at whatever was our usual and regular rate? Which was what, by the way? But not to worry, he'd made them promise to pay cash up front, and they were all really great guys, really: gentlemen and scholars, though tough on pledges and heavy on the brew. And was my first name actually Grace, as in Saving or Amazing? Fact stranger than fiction!

Et cetera, at a mile a minute, the guy was so nervous and excited and maybe a bit beered-up himself. But he agreed to our fee per head, so to speak, and to my proposal to bring along a couple of my sisters to help service his brothers, if he'd pick us up at nine sharp at the Arundel Club, near the ASTC campus, and have us back by one A.M. latest, as we had heavy studying to get done before our Monday classes.

And boyoboy, Listener, did *that* ever turn him on! What were we majoring in? What did we think of our profs at ASTC? Were we taking any literature courses, and what had we read lately that really blew us away? It was all Grace could do to get him off the phone and into his frat buddy's car to come fetch us in time for our date.

"Which, however, he did, on the dot, with his Marine-vet brother at the wheel; and where *that* one was all wise-guy winks and raunchy jokes, Pledge Manny was as flustered and courteous as if we were three debutantes being escorted to a coming-out party."

A lanky, bespectacled, red-haired, and freckle-faced nineteen-year-old he was, Listener, from the western Maryland mountains, on full scholarship at MDU and green as those Allegheny hills in May about most things social, sexual, and even academic. But a quick learner, as Gracie mentioned earlier, with a drunkard's thirst in all three of those departments.

"Speaking of which—I mean *threes? . . .*"

He was so wowed by there being three of us, and by the Mason-Dixon/Mason-Dickson coincidence, and my being named Grace, that by the time we hit the highway north for MDU he was already calling us his Three Graces—

Like the ones in the myths, which back then we-all were just learning about . . .

—and right away he names Thelma "Thalia" and Aggie "Aglaia," like them, and starts filling our ears with how, in his opinion, the Hell Week pledge tasks, with their go-find-thises and figure-out-thats, are a sort of undergrad version of stuff that the old-time heroes like Odysseus and Aeneas had to do: descents into the underworld, quests and ordeals and like that. And since what those hero types were really *after was capital-K Knowledge—like who they truly are, and how to get where they're supposed to go and do what they're destined to do when they get there?—it was sort of appropriate for college freshmen to reenact that Heroic Quest business as they began their own, didn't we think? And please excuse him for rattling on about this Greek myth stuff: It was on account*

of the coincidence that while he was learning the Greek alphabet, the way all MDU frat pledges had to do, he happened also to be reading Homer and Company in his freshman lit survey courses and getting hooked on all that great stuff, though he hadn't chosen a major yet because he couldn't make up his mind what he wanted to be when he grew up—maybe because he didn't really know yet who he was, *you know? And we should forgive him for hogging the mike so, when what he really wanted was to hear about our paying our way through college the way we were, which he thought was twice as heroical as anything he and his Hell Week pals were doing.*

"And didn't he flip when Gracie said he should make that *thrice* as heroical instead of *twice*, 'cause she'd noticed in our own lit classes that things in those old-time stories usually come in threes, whether it's the Graces and the Fates and such or the number of heads on that monster-dog Whatsisname, that guards the gates of Hades . . ."

Just about creamed his chinos at that, Manny did, and then perched on his knees in the passenger seat like a five-year-old—

"Like a *three*-year old—"

—to talk to the three of us in the back and see how many three-things we could come up with, from Goldilocks's bears to Dante's Hell, Purgatory, and Paradise.

Which Listener will remember are the three books of The Divine Comedy, *written in three-line stanzas, which Aggie gets the same A-plus for remembering now as Manny gave her for coming up with it then, especially the* terza rima *bit, all of it echoing the three-in-one Holy Trinity. Meanwhile, the driver-guy is rolling his eyes and shaking his crewcut head and telling Manny to pass the fucking Budweiser for God's sake and change the subject? By then we're in the city, in the blocks of rowhouses near the MDU campus, which is where most of the students live and the frat houses are, and we pull up to one that has two big Greek letters over the door, the left one like an upside-down capital V—which is actually their L, lambda—and the other like a right-side-up capital Y, which is upsilon, their U.*

As Manny happily explains to us, until smart-ass "Thalia" tells him the lambda looks to her like a pair of wide-open legs, and smart-ass Yours-Truly-"Aglaia" says that if that one has her legs open, the other one must have hers closed, which is no way to make a living. And then our driver—Bob, I believe his name was?—finally joins the fun by saying, "That chick's legs aren't closed; she's upside down with 'em spread wide open," and Manny says, "Welcome to Lambda Upsy-daisy, girls" as he hands us out of the car, and Gracie says, "Ten bucks a head to dine at the Y, guys," and in we go.

In we went, and out we came by midnight, nearly four hundred to the good, if that's the right word for it, having scored nearly a score of Lambda Upsies at our twenty-dollar group-rate special—

Including a couple of first-timers too nervous to get it up and a couple of old hands too drunk to; but nobody asked for a refund, so we gave 'em rain checks. Gents and scholars indeed, those guys, serenading us from downstairs while we turned our tricks in three separate third-floor bedrooms. *Gentleman songsters off on a spree . . .*

"Doomed to get laid by the Graces three?"

Who then gratefully rewarded Pledge Dickson with a freebie Threebie to add to his catalogue of triples: a stunt not to be found in his old-time myths. We improvised it on the spot, as I remember, having had a few beers ourselves by that time.

"And what Manny couldn't manage, we managed for him. Put *that* in your oral history, Junior, since Cindy saw fit not to in her novella-thing: your pop's first pop."

Which so shot his maiden wad that some other brother—the least plastered one we could locate—drove us home in exchange for another little trick en route.

And tired and sore and two-thirds sozzled as we ourselves were by then, we douched and showered, set the alarm, hit the books bright and early next morning, and got our weekend schoolwork done on time.

Which just about wraps up Episode One of our connection with Manfred Senior as a freshman. Which laid the foundation—

"In a manner of speaking—"

—for all that followed: his whole fucking career, I guess.

Also in a manner of speaking. And since there's not tape enough left on this cassette for us to start the next chapter, let's close this one by adding that Manny and his pals invited us back a few times that semester and the next, separately and together, until MDU got wind of it and cracked down on Lambda Upsilon, and the brothers lost their lease on the row-house. "Dickson's Masons," they used to call us.

And once we'd gotten him started on that business of Threes and Y's, and said what we'd said about those two Greek letters, Manny notebooked everything we told him as if we were one of those whatchacallum oracles. Philadelphic?

"Delphic Orifices, maybe?"

Not only siblings, but sibyls. And this was before the guy had decided or discovered who he was! But in his second year at MDU—and Thelma's at ASTC, and Aggie's and my junior

year there—he took up with a girl at Western Maryland College that he'd known from high school: the one he wound up marrying as soon as they both graduated. And since we sibyl types were still paying our freight in our particular way, it's no surprise that he didn't introduce us to his fiancée—that's your mom-to-be, Junior—or seek us out for more input, shall we say.

So we all commenced from our respective alma maters and went our separate if not quite equal ways—

"Some of us even went *straight,* once our last tuition bill was paid . . ."

—while some others found ourselves hooked on hookering, *faute de mieux.* But that's another story.

To be told another time, maybe, on another tape, before Cindy-Ella beats us to it with another novella à clef: how at least one ex-Mason reconnected with a much-changed Dickson. Let's close this one with a bit of oral oracularity for Junior-boy: that famously cryptic dedication of The Fates, *which the lit-crit types have read as a salute to everything from the classical Muses as literary architects to the secret fraternal order of Freemasonry.*

Try it orally with us, Manny-boy, and one more mystery will be demystified. All together now: one . . . two . . .

"To the Gracious Masons, who lent me—"

[End of tape.]

TAPE 3

. . . *their rears:* another Dickson triple-entendre lost in transcription, Listener, not to mention in translation.

"Like *wise.*"

At least one of which not even Grace is sure about: that

queer Y-on-its-side that marks the last book of Manny's trilogy.

Though she has her hunches. Your dad himself would never talk seriously about things like that, Junior, especially in later years. Depending on his mood—which more and more came to mean his booze intake, after MDU sacked him—he'd say something like, "You and I are the oracles, doll, not the commentators," or "Let's leave footnotes to the kinds of assholes who fired me."

"Like you-know-who, Junie-boy."

Not fair, Thelma: The kid's father gets booted when a conservative English Department finds they've got a nontenured Henry Miller on the faculty. His parents' marriage crashes, and his mom probably fills the kid's ears with made-up tales of his dad's fuck-arounds and orgies, which Manny's not there to deny 'cause he's out wrecking his liver. No wonder the kid's neutered! My Cindy and her brother were luckier, poor kids, having their pissed-off dad conveniently drop dead.

Amen. But "made-up tales," you said?

For the record, Junior, your pa may've been less than a model parent (likewise your ma, I'd bet my butt), but he was neither the big-time cocksman that some of his detractors and admirers alike have made him out to be, nor the fantasizing jerk-off that some others have maliciously proposed. In my own not-uninformed opinion, M. D. Senior was a man of no more than average libido, more curious *than lecherous or lustful, and more fixated on his freaking Threes and Y's and capital-Q Quests—not to mention language and storytelling—than on literal cunts and cocks.*

"I'll second that."

And I'll third it—though Thelm and I never came to know him the way Gracie did.

"'Came to know him . . .' Wait'll Junior goes to work on *that* line!"

What *I* suspect, girls, is that while J-boy's declared objective is to restore his dad's critical reputation (now that the guy's doubtless long since dead), his actual motive might be to get even with him for not having been a better father. Piss on his ashes, et cet?

"Amen to that, Aggie: Intentionally or not, that's what any quote *critical reappraisal* unquote of his will likely do, given where its author's coming from."

Ergo, guys, our Corrective Oral Testimony, if we ever get around to it before we've used up all three tapes. That sidewise Y, by the way—that Manny used for space-breaks and such right through the Atropos *novel?—might be like* scissors, *mightn't it, whatever else it stands for? She being the Fate who snips the thread that Clotho spins and Lachesis measures out . . .*

Score another for sister Grace, maybe. *I* always think of it as some Gracious-Mason type lying on her side and lifting her leg while "lending her rear"—but that's horny old me.

"If a mere former gynecologist's assistant can presume to add her reading to an ex–English teacher's and an ex–porn queen's, I'd say you're both right. The bitch-lady heroine of *Atropos* figuratively cuts her artist-lover's nuts off, no? Fucks him over till he can't get it up with the muses? Cindy's *Wye*-story comes close to saying that."

A-plus for Thelma Mason! And now watch us get some history done: Having whored our way cum laude *to our bachelor's degrees—*

"So to speak."

—two-thirds of us put sex-for-hire behind us after graduation.

Also so to speak—Yours-Truly-Agatha being the naughty third third.

But even she *quit being a hooker pure and simple, excuse the adjectives. Having been a drama major and varsity gymnast at Arundel State, she took those talents and her others up to NYC and later out to LA, to try her luck at modeling and actressing . . .*

Where she dropped her drawers in what she hoped were the right talent offices and undressing rooms, and actually managed to score a few photo shoots and bit parts. But then found her true métier—I believe the word is?—in Smutsville.

"You used to tell us it was the gymnastic aspect that appealed to you."

Manny even used that line—somewhere in Lachesis, *was it? On with your story, Ag.*

What's to tell? Unlike my straighter sisters, I never got to be anybody's wife or mother. Had a couple hundred lovers but never lucked into capital-L Love. Came closest with a more-or-less-lesbian colleague in my more-or-less-lesbian phase, but that didn't last either. Got too old for the porn game and worked as a talent scout for a while, till I learned I was scouting young illegal-immigrant Latinas to be flat-out *putas.* Put all that behind me in my forties and moved back east, where my better twin steered me to an M.Ed. degree and a job coaching gym and dramatics to the girls of Severn Day School.

Which in its innocence never made a better appointment: absolutely first-rate coach, teacher, and all-'round moral compass for her students.

"Because she'd been around the proverbial block and knew which alleys to avoid. But try to tell that to the SDS trustees, if Gracie's husband had blown the whistle on us as he threatened to."

Not to get too *far ahead of our story, while Aggie's off hustling the Big Apple and La-La Land, frisky Thelma finishes* her *degree, turns a few more tricks to pay for summer-school courses in secretarying, then goes straight and lands a good job as receptionist-slash-secretary-slash-assistant to a handsome young gynecologist in Baltimore . . .*

"A scrupulous practitioner, Listener, who would never *think* of taking liberties with his patients, but who—like me, once my tush was off the rental market—enjoyed sex with any willing, good-looking, lively, and reasonably discreet *non* patient, the way some other types enjoy workouts in the gym or Saturday-night dances at their country club."

Read all about it in *Clotho,* folks, where Manny calls her "Thalia" . . .

"Within a month after I was hired, Doctor Weisman and I were getting it on (never during office hours), and found we had so much else in common that we got married the following year, with the understanding that in our house, infidelity would mean *cheating* on one's spouse, not occasional mate-swapping among friends for the fun of it. And fun we had, folks, dear Sammy and I, till our luck ran out in the swinging nineteen-high-sixties. We half believed we were inventing open marriage! And thought it was super-cool for me to keep my maiden name. Tell the rest of it for me, Gracie."

The mercifully short version: Husband dies young of galloping lung cancer (we all still smoked like chimneys in those days), leaving bereft widow with a son, Benjy—slow-witted, obese, resentful, ungovernable, and altogether parasitic, in his outspoken twin aunts' opinion—who makes a misery of his mom's middle years until he piles up her Pontiac in a

DUI accident on the Baltimore Beltway, killing himself, two drinking buddies, and the innocent driver he was passing on the right at ninety miles an hour on a rainy March night in 1973.

To which his aunt Aggie would add—if I may, Thelma?—that once our wiped-out kid sister had closed that chapter of her life, she took a deep breath, quit punishing herself for her late son's problems, rediscovered the sense of humor and *joie de vivre* that'd been in cold storage since her good Doc Sam first took sick, and was a life-saving aid and comforter to Grace and me when *our* shit hit the fan at Severn Day School in the mid-seventies.

That's the century's *mid-seventies, Listener: our mid-forties, when a certain Ned Forester found and read his wife's private diaries from back in her college years—as I believe got mentioned earlier?—and her later notebooks on* The Fates.

"Self-righteous asshole."

Pillar of the community, in most folks' opinion, who'd believed his wife to be the same.

Whose wife *was* the same, we happen to know, for the twenty-plus years of their courtship and marriage, including the period of her reconnection with Manfred Dickson: a totally innocent reconnection, for which her only blame was keeping it secret from her husband lest he misunderstand and disapprove.

"As he damned well would've, for sure. Tell it, Gracie."

If I can, with apologies to my loyal and talented daughter for correcting here her fictionalized version. We lit-teacher types tend to think that the capital-A Authors whose stuff we teach must've been called to their vocation by some life-changing experience like discovering a particular book or mentor who helps them find their voice and their subject matter. And no doubt something like that's the case more often than not (it certainly was with "C. Ella Mason," as shall be seen). Even Manny, remember, when we Three-Wayed him back there at Lambda Upsilon, had been studying with some first-rate profs at MDU and chugalugging literature, history, and philosophy the way he and his frat buddies were downloading kegfuls of Pabst and Budweiser. But when our paths recrossed in '55, half a dozen years after our first get-together, he swore it was that Hell Week scavenger hunt that'd turned Manny the who-knows-what into Manfred F. Dickson the budding novelist. He didn't doubt that we all rewrite our pasts as we go along—maybe professional storytellers especially? But his *version of the Story of His Life, he swore, was that the coincidence of us Masons and Dicksons "coming together" at Mason-Dixon, along with the "Mythic Quest crapola," as he himself called it, and all those "Threebies," had so energized and focused his imagination that he'd been churning out paragraphs and pages of scenes and characters and plot situations ever since, as fast as he could hunt-and-peck 'em on his hand-me-down Underwood.*

By the time I tell of, when he and I were every bit of twenty-five years old, he was already three years married to Miz Western Maryland aforementioned and had a two-year-old son (named guess what). Like my Cindy all these years later, he'd published a handful of shall-we-say experimental short stories in obscure little lit mags and an unsuccessful "trial-run" first novel, as he called it (already out of print, and its small-press publisher out of business), and had a second one going the rounds in New York that neither he nor his agent was optimistic about. What's more, to pay the rent he was currently adjunct-professoring at . . . guess where? Arun-

del State College, as it was calling itself then! In his busyness at discovering and exploring his voice and his medium—plus all the distractions of teaching and husbanding and fathering—the particular circumstances of his original "Summons to Adventure," as the myth people call the Hero's wake-up call, had not been forgotten, by any means, but were somehow sidetracked in his imagination as if waiting to be renoticed and finally Understood. Believe it or not, he told me, it wasn't until he'd wangled that ASC appointment (which took a bit of wangling, as he had neither a Ph.D. nor any scholarly publications to his credit, just those three or four avant-garde stories and that flop of an oddball first novel) that he remembered exactly why *those Mason chicks had been doing what they did back in '48/'49, and which institution of higher education they'd been shagging their way through.*

"Whereupon . . . Bingo!"

Whereupon maybe not yet Bingo, but for sure By Golly. And he being just then both between projects and, he strongly felt, between the unimpressive First Phase of his writerly career and what he was convinced and determined would be the literary fireworks of Phase Two, he'd not only dug up and reexamined all the notes (and diagrams) that he'd made half a dozen years past, after our Lambda Upsy-daisy gig, but looked us up in the college's alumni directory (just as Junior did, forty-five years later), resolved to find out what had happened to his Three Graces since then: what we were up to these days, and how we *remembered that fateful night.*

Note the adjective, folks.

*Indeed. Because what Manny was calling his Second Quest, or the search for his Original Muses, was already part and parcel of the magnum opus that was beginning to take shape in his imagination—*magna opera, *I guess, since he knew already it would be a triple-decker . . .*

"Et cetera. All this, mind you, in a *letter,* Listener, addressed to Mrs. Grace Forester care of Severn Day, not to intrude on her domestic privacy. It was almost as long a letter as Junior's, but with a different tone entirely."

Courteous and discreet like Junie's, not to embarrass its recipient with past history in her present position. But relaxed, good-humored, and friendly: the voice of a flesh-and-blood human being. Nobody who didn't happen to know that item of our résumé could've guessed it from his letter. Which, by the way, he signed *Fred* over his typewritten *Manfred F. Dickson.* An inside joke, we learned later.

Anybody reading that letter would've thought at most that we four must have known one another from college days. And inasmuch as "Fred"'s project-in-the-works had to do with that particular time and place—post–World War Two America, the age of the A-bomb, the wearing out of Modernism, et cet—he had reason to believe that an interview or two with the former Grace Mason (and perhaps with her lively sister-graces "Aglaia" and "Thalia" as well, if I would kindly direct him to them) could be of considerable value to his researches. Might we meet, at any time and place of my convenience? Just say the word, he said, and he would quote "drop everything" unquote . . .

"Another Manny-tease, obviously. But *only* a tease, Junior, because when Gracie met your dad for lunch not long after, at what passed for a faculty club in those days at ASC—and then when *I* did some interview sessions with him a while later, and Aggie some time after that—the Manfred F. Dickson that we re-met was not about to drop his pants, for example, for any of us. Not even when Aggie and I, for old times' sake, as much as invited him to."

Which wouldn't've bothered Thelma's open-minded, open-marriage hubby—

"Don't forget open-*flied*—"

—which her open-armed and open-ended gynecologist hubby wouldn't've minded at all . . .

"Sammy mind? He'd've applauded! He knew my whole story and loved me for it, bless him."

And Yours Truly, the Porn Pro, sad to say, had nobody to be unfaithful *to.* Our point being that while the author of *The Fates* has been called, with some justice, both an erotomane and an egomane—are those the right terms, Teach?

They'll serve, and I have more to say on that subject. After you.

. . . he never once, in the seven years of our reconnection, made improper advances to any of the three of us; not even when one or two of us suggested same. And those suggesters never included Mrs. Ned Stuffed-Shirt Forester. Tell it, Grace.

Well: What Junior needs to know (likewise Mason-Dixon U. and Arundel U. and the Library of Congress, to all of whom I'll be sending copies of my transcriptions of these tapes for their M. F. Dickson Archives, present or future, in case Junior tosses or edits the originals) is that his dad's egomania, narcissism, whatever bad name it's called by, was in my *humble opinion not self-*love *at all, but a particular kind of self-*absorption *fairly common among artist types, though not a vocational prerequisite. Even "self-absorption" and "self-centeredness" are only half accurate (as my daughter will testify from her own experience), since what Manny's "self" was absorbed with and centered on—what for better or worse took precedence over his marriage and family and academic responsibilities, not to mention over friends and community and the wider world—wasn't his ego, in any vain sense of that term: It was his* work.

"His *fucking* work."

Another misleading adjective, Thelm, if Bernbridge Manor's resident authority on that activity may put in a word here about that word. Somebody mentioned *erotomania* a while ago—me, probably, because what's on my mind is either Gracie's or Manny's reminding us, way back then, that since Erato was the Greeks' muse of love poetry, capital-E Eratomania can mean being hooked on that muse and her medium, not necessarily on sex *per se.* Am I being too literary for an ex-pornie?

Maybe, but not for an Arundel State cum laude *and ex–Severn Day drama coach. It was the* idea *of women and their bodies that obsessed Manny: all our little nooks and crannies, what could be done with them and said about them, and what they could be made to stand for—*

Or to put up with . . .

—of which our actual PTTs—pussies, tits, and tushies?—were just inspiring reminders.

"Right on. What it used to remind *me* of, changes changed, was a certain husband of mine's endless fascination with every aspect of female plumbing, wiring, and the rest: a *professional* fascination, I was going to say, but it wasn't *merely* professional, by a long shot. Sammy used to say that he became a gynecologist because he'd liked playing doctor with his little-girl classmates in first grade. So he becomes a top-flight gynecologist who can't keep his fly zipped with any willing, uninfected chick who's not one of his patients. Who's to say what's cause and what's effect?"

While Manny, on the contrary, did *keep his fly zipped the whole time we were working together on* The Fates. *He wasn't interested in* committing *adultery, either of the Passionate Extramarital Love Affair kind or Doc Sam's General Screw-*

ing Around. It was the concept *of Sexual Infidelity, like the concept of Love, that turned his imagination on. Don't think of him as whacking off with his left hand while scribbling sentences with his right, Junior, or as fantasizing about his fictional heroines while humping your mom—*

Which is not to say he mightn't have done both, at least now and then . . .

"But Gracie's right, as usual: The point is that literal sex was never his *point.*"

Never his whole *point, and seldom his main point. Manny just couldn't get over the* ingenuity *of Evolution, coming up after millions of years not only with sperm and eggs and cocks and cunts, but with peacock tails and seventeen-year-cicada mating swarms, along with love poems, wedding ceremonies, G-strings, and string bikinis—*

Named after a certain South Pacific atoll, our younger listeners may need reminding, where the US of A tested nuclear weapons from 1946 right up to the year when Manny published *Clotho.* You could say that *The Fates* are a kind of literary fallout from that radioactive period.

"Or that sister Aggie could've been a fine English teach like her twin."

Our point being that there's a shitload more than S-E-X in that trilogy of his.

Amen to that. The great ones in any medium get to the bottom of things through some unlikely doors indeed: Monet's haystacks, Joyce's Bloomsday, Picasso's Demoiselles d'Avignon—

"And M. F. Dickson's *Gracious Masons, who lent him their* et ceteras."

Meaning truly our *ears,* Listener, this time around. Especially Gracie's—who'll now maybe homestretch this oral history?

"A-u-r-a-l history? Sorry there, guys . . ."

Here we go: It's been said already that Manny and I worked closely together from '55 through '62/'63, first while he was part-timing at ASC and then while he was happily doing the same back at his alma mater, on the strength of Clotho's *acceptance for publication in '57 but before it became a* succès de scandale. *I want to get it on record that* he *did all the composing—in his nearly illegible ballpoint-penmanship on stacks of white legal pads, which I then deciphered as best I could and typed up for him to revise and rewrite: draft after draft, year after year—*

With a fair amount of editing by his frustrated-writer typist, over and above her quote-unquote *deciphering* of his hieroglyphics—

"Not to mention the raw material, excuse the expression, that the three of us filled his eager ears with. We all did our bit."

We did indeed. But let's be clear on that editing *bit, Ag: I made comments and suggestions aplenty, some of which he picked up on and others not. But the critics who've claimed or implied that I as much as* coauthored *Manny's books—*

"Not to mention at least one who'd like to believe that you *ghostwrote* 'em for him—"

—have their critical heads up their professorial asses, and that's the end of that.

But not the end of your story. *Our* story.

Not quite its end, but its end's beginning. Let Listener be reminded that the Fates *novels came out at three-year intervals, commencing with* Clotho *in '57 and* Lachesis *in '60—both from a small, notorious English-language press in Paris that specialized in Seriously Naughty Lit—before the complete trilogy was published with much fanfare by a New York trade house in November 1963. The coincidence of its appear-*

ance and President Kennedy's assassination was a factor in The Fates' *becoming one more icon of the Johnson/Nixon/ Vietnam War high sixties in rock-and-roll America, along with sit-ins and love-ins, sideburns and ponytails, bongs and bell-bottoms and the rest. But even before* Atropos *was in print,* Clotho *and* Lachesis *had gotten their author hounded out of academia as a pornographer and divorced by his wife, who moved cross-country with ten-year-old Junior and holed up somewhere out in Oregon. Poor Manny—hailed in some quarters, condemned or merely dismissed in others—ended our seven-year working relationship with not much more than a shrug and a thank-you-ma'am.* He *holed up in a mountain cabin back in his native western Maryland and commenced his descent into alcohol, drugs, and cranky hermithood like some combination of Jack Kerouac and J. D. Salinger, rumored to be still writing, though no longer publishing, until his mysterious disappearance "out west" at the decade's end.*

Which we'll return to, folks—having established, we trust, that while the capital-E Erotic was our "Fred" 's characteristic mode, medium, and material, it was seldom his real subject. The guy was no prude, but that old Lambda Upsy-daisy of ours was a notable exception to a sexually restrained, contentedly monogamous life.

"Poor shmuck—and that's enough about *that.* Gracie?"

Poor dear *shmuck. So he kisses me goodbye in the winter of '62/'63—modestly, mind you, on the forehead—and thanks me for all my help. For which he'd been paying me ten percent of his meager royalties, I should've said earlier: another little secret I kept from my husband, like my notebooks on our collaboration. Then, when the American edition of the trilogy brought in some serious money, Manny's ex claimed most of it as back alimony and child support, and he signed it over to her.*

"Shmuck shmendrick shlimazl!"

It's who he was, Thelma, for better or worse.

Following which, he disappears in an alcoholic haze out west . . .

With Elvis-like reports of his being spotted in San Francisco's Haight-Ashbury or some hippie commune in Santa Fe or on the road with Ken Kesey's Merry Pranksters. No trace of further manuscripts in the abandoned cabin, but now and then some lit mag would come out with a Dicksonish piece that it claimed had been sent in under Manny's name from Taos or Tijuana, but with no cover note or street address, and which the critics would then debate the authenticity of. Likewise the occasional fragments and even a couple of whole story scripts that someone would claim to've turned up in a desk drawer at Arundel State or Mason-Dixon U.—a gimmick that Cindy makes good use of in her Wye *novella. I could've identified his handwriting right off, but those scripts were always typed (not by me), so who knows? Some of the ones I saw in print sounded less unlikely to me than others—but by the time they surfaced, in the early 1970s, I was busy with my own troubles.*

Weren't we all. But yours first, Grace: the non-Cindy-Ella version.

Listener needs to be reminded that when Manny first relocated me back in '55 and asked for my "input" on his project-in-the-works, I didn't mention it to my husband for fear he'd find out how his wife had paid her way through college. When our reconnection grew into a regular working relationship, my line with Ned and our kids was that I'd always secretly aspired to write a novel, and was determined to give it a try in what little time a prep school wife and mother can spare from her main responsibilities. And they were great about leaving Mommy undisturbed when she was typing away in her study or "doing her homework" in the Severn Day or Arundel State libraries. During most of those seven years I was seldom actually with *Manny for more than an hour maybe once a week, when either I'd meet him on campus at ASC to pick up his latest batch of scribbling and go through my annotated typescript from the week before, or he'd stop by the faculty mailroom at Severn Day after he'd shifted up to MDU. In the* Atropos *period, after he'd been sacked by the university but before he holed up in the Allegheny hills, we'd have our little conferences in an Annapolis restaurant booth. And maybe half a dozen times, I admit, I met him in some motel or other where he was camping after his wife threw him out, or just staying over to get some research done.*

"Some research . . ."

Okay, I know what Listener's thinking—same as Ned did when he found my diaries. And I grant it sounds like we were going at it. But as Cindy makes clear in her story, it was really more like modeling for life drawing classes in art school. If Manny's mock–Mythic Hero "Fred," for instance (the male lead in the Fates *novels, as in* Wye*), is having himself an early-midlife crisis—as he does in* Atropos *after dodging the Korean War draft and realizing that he and his wife are evolving in different directions—and one of his colleagues' wives happens to hit on him, and he's reminded of some crazy sex he had back in college days with a girl who looked like a younger version of this one, and Manny needs to describe exactly how Fred feels being in a motel room at age forty with a thirty-year-old married woman naked on all fours, and worrying that he might not get it up for her because of the novelty of it all, dot dot dot? But I swear on Bill Clinton's testicles that* I never had sex with that man: *I merely might as well have, since I told my damn diary all about us, chapter and verse.*

No comment.

"Ditto—except what if Mister Manny needed to know exactly how it felt to Mister Fred there to ball the lady's brains out?"

No comment. What I want to get said is that after '62, when the Dickson-Mason connection was history, it was a real relief for me to abandon my make-pretend writing ambitions and get back to full-time wifing, mothering, and schoolteaching. I loved *Ned Forester, damn it, different as we were in too many ways. And our kids meant the world to me.*

I beg to disagree with that "make-pretend": Not only did you teach literature and composition for a living, and fill umpteen diaries with your take on everything from losing your cherry at age sixteen to posing bare-assed for Manfred Dickson in a Howard Johnson motel room at age thirty; you also "edited," quote/unquote, every page he wrote for seven years! Thelma and I supplied him with a certain amount of information—

"Not to mention a few demos here and there—"

But *you* were muse and editor rolled into one.

"So to speak."

So okay, you didn't *write* Manny's books. But *The Fates* would never have gotten themselves written without you.

For better or worse, thanks, depending on where you're coming from. Junior himself half wishes he could prove I wrote them, we half suspect, so he could shoot down his big bad daddy's main claim to fame—except that there would go his *only fame-claim, too. But my diaries made it clear which of us was the novelist and which the typist/editor, as does dear Cindy's* Wye.

"Pity Junie didn't get to read 'em. And the world."

A painful subject, so let's get done with it. I never kept those diaries hidden, Listener: neither the ones that Manny found so useful, from back in our tuition-earning days, nor the later ones from our reconnection. They were lined up on a bookshelf in my study, where anybody from the kids to the housecleaner could pick them up. But they were *under lock and key, sort of, because like a lot of schoolgirls I'd started with the kind that have a little locking tab to keep them private, and I kept on using that kind, half out of habit, half as a joke. Ned and the kids used to tease me about "Mommy's deep dark secrets." I even made the little brass keys into a charm bracelet, usually tucked away in my jewelry box, and never imagined that et cetera.*

And to this hour I don't know quite what prompted Ned to fish out that bracelet one day in December of 1973 and unlock those locks. He'd been in bed for a few days with the flu and got bored lying there alone in the house while the kids and I were in school; said he noticed that key-bracelet on my dresser (possible, but not likely) and thought what the hell, no harm in just taking a peek—and that was that. Just as the Arab oil embargo and economic recession of '73 ended the American sixties, of which The Fates *had become an emblem, Ned's reading those diaries was the end of the world as Grace Mason Forester had known and enjoyed it. Twenty years of contented marriage and eighteen of happy motherhood down the toilet, not to mention my job and poor Aggie's at Severn Day.*

What happened, Listener—contrary to the "C. Ella Mason" version—was that Outraged Hubby threatened to put those diaries in evidence if Grace contested their immediate separation and divorce—although of course he'd prefer not to, to spare all hands the embarrassment of everybody's learning that nice Missus Forester is an ex-hooker who later shacked up for seven adulterous years with a famous dirty-book writer.

Which I didn't, but who'd believe me?

"*I* still think you should've called his bluff and said, So go public, asshole. He had as much to lose as you did."

I couldn't do that, Thelm, for the kids' sake. And for Ned's, too. I'd loved *him, damn it, and what he'd found out about me cut him to the quick. I didn't want him publicly humiliated too.*

So the bastard insists on divorce for irreconcilable differences, full custody of the kids, and Gracie's and my resignation from Severn Day, where he was sure we'd been corrupting our students' morals: otherwise he'd blow the cover on my porn-queen past along with Grace's diaries. But if we agreed to his terms, he promised to destroy the diaries, keep mum about our naughty résumés, and make a generous alimony settlement.

"And Listener should understand that the matter of Grace's visitation rights with their kids was academic anyhow, so to speak, since Ned Junior was about to take off for Princeton and Cindy was a fifth-former already at Severn Day. Even so, I think you should've dared him to go ahead and cover the whole family with shit."

Nope. And as things turned out, I'm glad I didn't—rough as it was for Ag and me to quit teaching, pretending that we were burned out.

Plausible enough for Grace, who'd been at it heart and soul for twenty-plus years. But I was only two years into the best job I ever had! As for how things turned out . . .

Poor Ned.

"Would you stop it already with the Poor Ned?"

No. What poor Ned had learned about me literally broke his heart. Cindy has him jump out of his high-rise office window—her way of getting even with him, I suppose. But in fact her dad died of a coronary, Listener, the very next year, at age fifty.

"On the fifteenth hole of his club's golf course, and in the opinion of some of us, his *coup de grâce,* excuse my French, was Tricky Dick Nixon's disgrace and resignation after Watergate, on top of all the rest."

So there went those cushy alimony payments, with which my sweet sorrowful sis had been helping me out while we both scratched around for new jobs. But she regained full custody of two well-off kiddies indeed, with their dad's estate added to their trust funds, and their mom in charge of the show till they reached twenty-one.

By when I'd long since explained to them what Mom and Dad's split had really been about.

"And they were totally cool with it, bless 'em! Sort of *proud* of their mom and dear aunties for having worked our way through college the way we did. They even thought it was cool that Aunt Aggie had been a porn star: 'No wonder she's the best gym coach ever!' Cindy told me: 'All those acrobatics!' "

And young Neddie—who'd switched his major at Princeton from Business to Art History as soon as his dad wasn't around to say no—was as wowed as his kid sister by the news that their mom had not only *known* the late, great Manfred F. Dickson, but had actually worked with him on *The Fates* for all those years! That news was what turned Cindy-Ella into a writer.

Into a commercially unsuccessful writer, she likes to say, who refuses to write "chick lit" and who defines the novella, her favorite form, as a story too long to sell to a magazine and too short to sell to a book publisher, bless her. Anyhow, the coast being clear, Ag and I were of course eager to get back to our teaching, both to pay the rent after my alimony stopped and because we were teachers to the bone. But our slots at Severn Day had been filled by young replacements whom we didn't want to bump, and we didn't have the Education credits that public school systems are fussy about. So in '76 I went to work as assistant librarian at Severn Day and then as head librarian when my boss retired: a post I held happily indeed for the next eighteen years, till I *retired at age sixty-five and my health gave out, as if on cue. As for Aggie . . . she'll speak for herself, and then Thelma likewise, before we're out of tape. Ag?*

Not much to tell. Less blessed in the résumé way than my twin, when Ned forced us out of teaching I supported myself with pickup jobs—like selling cosmetics and jewelry at Kmart and J. C. Penney—until Grace was reestablished at Severn and eased me back in to help coach drama, dance, and gym. When arthritis and emphysema sidelined me for keeps, we shared a nice apartment in Annapolis, not far from where we'd grown up, and I played housekeeper as best I could to earn my room and board till Gracie retired. It was like being kids again, only with separate bedrooms for us and a sleep sofa for overnight guests like Gracie's grown-up youngsters.

A luxury we never had as Navy brats, not to mention as womb-mates. And that's our story, folks, except for how we wound up as a threesome here in Bernbridge. Your ship, Thelma.

"Aye aye, Cap'n. I was the only Gracious Mason not damaged by our undergrad tuition-paying *per se* or by prick-head Ned Forester's reading all about it in Gracie's fucking diaries, as we call 'em. Between Doctor Sam and me, all that stuff had been a family joke: As I said, he was *proud* of me for it. And by the time Ned blew his whistle on the three of us, *my* world had ended twice already, at ages thirty-nine and forty-three: first with Sammy's death in the summer of '69 (wouldn't he have loved the idea of croaking in mid-*soixante-neuf!*) and then with poor Benjy's wipeout in the spring of '73. I doubt I'd have weathered those losses without my two sisters' support; helping them later through *their* bad time was downright therapeutic for me."

By then all three of us were back in the old hometown . . .

"Right. Benjy had needed so much looking after that I'd long since quit my job in Sam's office and had tried in vain to turn our son into a responsible kid. After Sammy died, it had been a relief as well as an economic necessity to sell our house in Baltimore, move into a condo, and go back to work for one of his ob/gyn colleagues. Early in '73 the guy shifted his practice down to Bowie, halfway between Annapolis and Washington, and for a few months I made the long commute so that Benjy could finish his senior year at Park School. But when he dropped out of school that February and piled up on the Beltway in March, at Grace and Aggie's urging I swapped the Baltimore condo for one in Annapolis, a quick shot from the new office, *et voilà:* Unhappy Fate had brought the three Fates happily together again."

Just in time for you to become the rescuer and us the rescued. Bless you for that.

Let me add that we were all in our forties by then, like Cindy and Neddie now: happy to be reunited but unhappy to be widows, divorcées, and never-marrieds; banged around by life but kept afloat by Thelma/Thalia's unfailing good humor —and none of us, for our separate reasons, much interested by then in finding another significant other. By the time the Great Diary Fallout was truly behind us, we were turning fifty, content with our new jobs and salvaged life situations, and independent except for our interdependency . . .

"A different kind of Three-Way from the classic model."

And the first Ph.D. dissertations were being written on Manny's Fates.

To all of which I would add that while Gracie and I especially, now that we were reinstalled at Severn Day, had to be super-discreet in the area of S-E-X, none of the three of us had yet abandoned such pleasures altogether. Had we?

Well: I *had, I guess—except for getting it off now and then with the handy-dandy gizmo that you guys gave me for my forty-fifth. But* you *had your little sessions with Carol Tucker, didn't you, Ag?*

A *very* well-to-do former student of ours, Listener, by then a trustee of Severn Day and thus not likely to spill our beans. She and I would get together in her hotel whenever she was in town for a board meeting. Sweet saucy If-You-Can't-Fuck-Her-Suck-Her Tucker: Erato's last stand. *Et tu,* Thalia?

"Me? Yes. Well: Widowhood took the zing out of Open Marriage, for sure. And I'm convinced that Ronald Reagan's election in 1980 brought on my early menopause, or at least a total loss of appetite in that department after age fifty. For the next dozen-plus years I got off on tennis and aerobics instead, until my back and knees gave out and I broke my hip in an escalator tumble at our nearby Nordstrom. And so at the tender age of seventy, here we are at Bernbridge-in-the-Boondocks, waiting to die."

Some of us more patiently than others. And how we wound up here is as follows: Gracie, s.v.p.?

Got it. As has been told, Aggie's early emphysema and the rest sidelined her circa *1979, when she was just turning fifty.*

Thelma and I were able to work into our sixties, until her failing joints nudged her into slightly early retirement from her doctor's office job and my reaching sixty-five prompted my very *reluctant goodbye to Severn Day. Which life change, I'm convinced, inspired my uterine cancer, cured by the timely removal of all that female plumbing that had so bemused both Doc Sam Weisman and Manny Dickson in their different ways. Have we mentioned, Junior, that* LIFE'S A BITCH, *as the bumper sticker says,* AND THEN YOU DIE, *if you're lucky enough to live so long? Meanwhile, however, it does have its moments, and the older and feebler we-all got—me especially, I guess—the more it seemed to us that our college days (you know what I mean) were the most eventful, the most memorable, the most* fun *time of our lives, in particular those Lambda Upsilon gigs with Manny and all that followed therefrom: his obsession with Y's and threesomes and mythic obstacle courses and scavenger hunts. We've loved our various mates and our children and our students and our work, but what we're most likely to be remembered for, if anything—whether thanks to Junior's biography-in-the-works or despite it—is our inspiration of Manfred Dickson's trilogy and our later input-sessions with him while he was writing it. As my Cindy-Ella of a daughter makes clear (rising from the ashes of her parents' divorce to turn smut into Art), that was* our *Place Where Three Roads Met.*

So what happened—if I may, Gracie?—was that when we reached the point where even housekeeping got to be more than the three of us could manage, and we needed ever more looking after, we scouted all the assisted-living kinds of places in the Baltimore/Washington/Annapolis area, and found enough pluses and minuses in every one to make the thing a tossup. So back and forth we went, literally and figuratively, until we were dizzy with indecision and getting on one another's nerves and about ready to just flip a coin, if we'd had an eight- or ten-sided coin. Then one fine day near the start of Bill Clinton's second term, Thelma came to our rescue by announcing . . . Thelm?

"By announcing, 'None of the above, girls: It's going to be Bernbridge Manor for us, way up in Bernbridge EmDee, where we don't know a frigging soul, and who cares, since most of our old friends are dead anyhow.' "

Thus spake Thalia, and we said, "Bernbridge? What's this Bernbridge? Why Bernbridge?" And she *said, "You nailed it, Gracie: Here's the Why." By which she meant both the* reason *why and the* letter *Y, as she showed us on the map.*

"Because once I'd thought of it, and the three of us, and our connection with Manny, I got as hooked on those Y's as he'd been—to the point where I actually looked to see whether there might be an assisted-living place somewhere on the Wye River, over on Maryland's Eastern Shore, where Clinton and Arafat and Netanyahu signed that Wye River Accord that led to zilch. As did my not-so-Heroic Quest? So then, just to get the damned decision decided, I checked out all such configurations within a fifty-mile radius of Annapolis, and *voilà!*"

Voilà indeed: the far northeast corner of the Old Line State, where the Mason-Dixon, appropriately, quits running east-west to divide Pennsylvania from Maryland, among other things, and turns ninety degrees south to divide Maryland from Delaware, while the line between Delaware and Pennsylvania shoots off northeastward in a great arc around Wilmington—a sort of loopy-looking lambda, to those inclined to see such things.

More exactly, our Bernbridge sits just a stone's throw from that three-way, on yet another one, where Route 896 drops south from Pennsylvania to the east end of the Mason-Dixon.

Just where it crosses that celebrated line at the curious conjunction that Aggie mentioned and continues southeastward into Delaware, a county road forks off southwestward into Maryland: a jim-dandy inverted Y like the one in Clotho, *superimposed on that state-line three-way out of* Lachesis*! My kids said, "Go for it, Mom!" Who could resist?*

And who gave a shit anyhow? Our life stories were all but told by then, through the second half of a century whose horrors we'd been spared, up to the commencement of another, which bids at best to be no better. Each of us had seen and done and been whatever, separately or together, and *hadn't* seen/done/been what we hadn't, for better or worse. So now we play Bernbridge bridge and bingo while we wait for our systems to finish failing—and who gives a shit, and why should they? What's it all been for?

Well, now, Aggie: pour l'art, *maybe? To've added a bit of spice to a certain Controversial Modern Classic and a not-bad-at-all spinoff novella, and now to shed a little light on the circumstances of their composition. Is that nothing?*

Yup.

"No! Unless Aggie's reached the point of feeling that capital-C Civilization itself is nothing."

I'm getting there. But I do still enjoy our glass of wine every night with dinner.

Then you're still welcomely on board, sis. And if the tape of our lives has almost run out, that means there may be enough left for a few last words. Your mike, Aggie.

Fuck it. And fuck *you,* motherfucking Junior, and your fucking father and his fucking hero-myth and his fucking books. Fuck everything—except my sisters.

Good girl, Ag: still aboard, even as our ship goes down. Thelma?

"Just want to add what only now occurred to me: that if

we think of Junior's tracking us down here at Bernbridge last month—which Cindy had given us advance warning of, Listener, after he'd tracked *her* down—as a *re*play of his father's tracking *us* down in Annapolis back in the mid-fifties, then that old reconnection with Manny Senior can be called the *fore*play of what we're doing now with Junior. Right?"

Amen.

I.e., fucking him over?

"And over and over. Over and out, Gracie."

—as we used to say to our quickie customers back in undergraduate days, Junior, as we rolled over when their five minutes were up. See *Lachesis,* page something-or-other. *Over and out, luv.* And then, *Next?*

So, Junior: Instead of "We who are about to die salute you," as the Roman gladiators used to say, it's "We who are on our last legs give you the finger." Unless, lad—what's too much to hope for, we suppose, but stranger things have happened in the history of inadequate parents and their screwed-up spawn—unless you somehow see fit to include an unedited transcript of these tapes in your big-shit three-decker critical biography of your old man. A kind of appendix, maybe?

"Scratch that, Grace: Appendixes can be surgically removed. What we've laid on you here, Junie, is no appendix: It's the heart and backbone of the story."

Its very cock and balls, if you know what we mean. Take us out, Grace.

Roger wilco. As I was saying—

EDITOR'S NOTE

At this point, the third of the three "Bernbridge" audiotapes—purportedly recorded at my urging by the elderly Mason sisters on 31 December 1999 and 1 January 2000

—ran out, and (the ladies evidently not realizing that there was unused footage remaining on Tapes 1 and 2) their scabrous three-way commentary on their alleged association with the late author of *The Fates* terminates abruptly in mid-sentence: not artfully, like the "ending" of *Finnegans Wake,* which circles back to its mid-sentence opening to complete the cycle of Eternal Recurrence which is that masterwork's Ground Theme, but unintentionally, leaving their potty-mouthed spiel unfinished like the *Atropos* volume of "my father"'s trilogy. One reasonably wonders why the harpy-in-chief, Ms. Grace Mason Forester, when she rewound, replayed, transcribed, and enlarged upon the trio's recorded conversation, didn't complete her closing statement, whether that statement was to be the sisters' nasty imprecation-in-progress against the present writer or their disillusioned *adieu* to the only historically significant aspect of their lives: their initial (unintended, accidental) inspiring of "my father" at a formative moment in his literary apprenticeship and their subsequent "input" (and, in Ms. Forester's case, stenographic and perhaps limited editorial assistance, to say no more) in the completion of his *chef d'oeuvre*—for both of which matters, to be sure, one has only their testimony, the ambiguous evidence of "C. Ella Mason"'s *Wye* novella, and that obscure, much-puzzled-over dedication of *The Fates:* "To the Gracious Masons, who . . ."*

The patient reader of this extended study, and especially of this appendix thereto, will have noted its author-editor's

* A dedication that remains puzzling despite my having identified the (decidedly *un-*)"Gracious Masons" and included in this appendix their characteristically ribald perversion of the phrase "their ears," since on the evidence of their testimony it was my father who eagerly lent *his* ears to their naughty glosses on, e.g., *lambda, upsilon,* and *trivium.*

occasional quotation marks around "my father," and may well have inferred their reason. Of my biological parentage I have no doubts: Readers who compare the several photographs herein of Manfred F. Dickson Sr. at his son's approximate present age and the jacket-flap mug shot of myself will not fail to note the unmistakable resemblance. But as prevailingly cordial, or at least civil, as our connection was through my boyhood, adolescence, and young manhood, I never felt *loved* by the father whom, per Evolution's heedless program, I loved helplessly, and whom I honor yet (as witness this years-long labor, now all but concluded), despite his lifelong indifference to, amounting to virtual rejection of, his only child. As if Oedipus, put out as an infant by his father, Laius, to die lest he grow up as foretold by Apollo to become a parricide, upon encountering years later that road-hogging old Theban at the Place Where Three Roads Meet, instead of killing him to clear his own path, had graciously yielded the right-of-way and then, belatedly realizing who the elderly stranger must be, had hurried after him (as I've done here in three long volumes), crying, like a character out of Kafka, "Father! Look! Your son, alive and well except for an unaccountably swollen foot! Your son, who craves only reunion, reconciliation, and the father I never had! Wait for me! I forgive you everything! Let's go on from here together!" But the oldster's wagon is gone already down that westward road, with not a backward glance from its heartless driver at its heartbroken pursuer. Who, unable despite all to embrace the uncaring sire whose shade still taunts, trudges behind on his own career-long Heroic Quest, from the outset knowing it to be in vain.

How tempting it has been, through the years of this monumental labor, to settle scores with that father-who-was-no-father—perhaps by repeating in parlous detail my mother's still-festering grievances from the latter years of their "mis-marriage," as she calls it, when she in her way like I in mine was sacrificed to his obsession with *The Fates*! Or by dwelling, in three-volume detail, upon the undeniable literary shortcomings of that trilogy, whose "controversial" aspects include more than its relentless, hyperbolical, ultimately tiresome eroticism! Or even to make the case that the work's real authorship should be credited (or debited) more to Grace Mason Forester than to M. F. Dickson Sr.—a man so lost in his preoccupations that it is arguably more a matter of *his* having perversely inspired *her* (a would-be novelist of sorts like her daughter, perhaps, but obliged to conceal her virtual authorship of *The Fates* lest her scandalized husband divorce her, as subsequently he did on lesser grounds) than vice versa!

Or even . . . (words fail me, as at the unended end of *Atropos* they failed its author-up-to-that-point) . . . to take the most sweepingly "Oedipal" revenge of all, by publishing this "appended" tape transcript and its appended Editor's Note separately from the three-volume critical corpus whose (vermiform!) Appendix it was meant to be—indeed, perhaps by publishing it *instead* of that obese, yet-to-be-completed corpus—and planting in it the seed (or worm) of insinuation that "my father," "Manfred F. Dickson" ("Sr."), and "his" trilogy *The Fates* are in fact finally fictions, the score-settling invention of a justly aggrieved virtual orphan whose lifelong, single-minded, but altogether futile endeavor to follow in his "father"'s footsteps has deprived him of any "meaningful" companionship except—take *this*, damned Dad!—playing King Oedipus indeed to a certain long-discarded Queen Jocasta, in a secret, Sphinx-guarded Thebes of our own devising!

Ha! There is no *Clotho,* Reader! No *Lachesis!* No *Atropos!* No Arundel or Mason-Dixon University, Severn Day School, or Bernbridge Manor! Nor any "Agatha/Aglaia," "Thelma/Thalia," or "Grace Mason Forester"! There is not, nor was there ever, any "M. F. Dickson Senior," nor (*ipso facto*) any M-F Junior! Figments all! Hollow, pathetic fictions!

There is only . . .

THE END

No: There is not even that. Not even that!

As I was saying . . .

Copyright © 20?? by "Fred"